"I'm surprised you remembered my name," Olivia teased Reese.

"Of course I remember your name."

"You didn't earlier."

"Well, I was focused on two small troublemakers. So my brain was occupied elsewhere. If you had kids you'd understand how easy it is to get side-tracked."

If she had kids—

I was a wife and mother once, her heart cried out. *Until my family was stolen from me.*

What would it be like to be part of a family again, to work with kids again, to find the connection that would make her part of something? Olivia longed to find out—but still feared some newspaper reporter would figure out who she'd been and run another story about her pitiful past.

Reese's sister Sara had been the first person Olivia had trusted in a very long time. And even Sara didn't know the whole truth.

The jury was still out on trusting Reese.

LOIS RICHER

likes variety. From her time in human resources management to entrepreneurship, life has held plenty of surprises. She says, "Having given up on fairy tales, I was happily involved in building a restaurant when a handsome prince walked into my life and upset all my career plans with a wedding ring. Motherhood quickly followed. I guess the seeds of my storytelling took root because of two small boys who kept demanding, 'Then what, Mom?'" The miracle of God's love for His children, the blessing of true love, the joy of sharing Him with others—that is a story that can be told a thousand ways and yet still be brand-new. Lois Richer intends to go right on telling it.

Twice Upon a Time
Lois Richer

Steeple
Hill®

Published by Steeple Hill Books™

STEEPLE HILL BOOKS

Steeple
Hill®

Recycling programs
for this product may
not exist in your area.

ISBN-13: 978-0-373-81401-5
ISBN-10:   0-373-81401-1

TWICE UPON A TIME

www.SteepleHill.com

Printed in U.S.A.

For the Holy Spirit, God's gift, doesn't want you to be afraid of people, but to be wise and strong, and to love them and enjoy being with them.

—II *Timothy* 1:7

This book is dedicated to dads who love when it isn't easy, try when they have no strength left and come running when you most need them.
Yours is a rich legacy.

Chapter One

I was that happy once.

Olivia Hastings slipped away from the crowd at the hilltop wedding reception to regain her peace of mind. She set her bridesmaid bouquet on a rock before wandering farther downhill and away from the laughing guests.

A few moments of solitude were all Olivia needed.

"We're not s'posed to come here."

That childish warning, barely audible, floated toward her on the soft summer wind, rousing her curiosity. The Woodward twins?

Olivia kept walking, stepping carefully around thistles as she followed the voices. The twins, Brett and Brady Woodward, were the bride's nephews. They'd taken part in a fundraiser Olivia had directed last month. The twins had stolen the show, though their father hadn't bothered to see it.

Reese Woodward was busy, his sister Sara claimed. Olivia thought he was *too* busy.

"Uncle Cade said he caught fish in here when he was a little boy."

The stream! Olivia picked up her pace downhill, over hillocks topped with cropped grass, not caring that her silk dress would probably be ruined.

Two four-year-old boys near water spelled disaster.

"I want to catch a fish."

"No, Brett. Uncle Cade said..."

His voice dissipated. Olivia strained, but couldn't see the boys. She glanced around to call for help and realized no one would hear above the wedding reception music. Anyway, the wind would carry her voice away. She'd have to manage on her own. Olivia felt certain that, given the love she'd witnessed the Woodward family lavish on the twins, one or another of Denver's famous wedding-planning family would soon come looking.

"Brett, you can't go in. Daddy said—"

"You boys get away from that water," Olivia yelled in her sternest tone, praying she wouldn't be too late. She stubbed her toe on a rock and bit down to smother her cry as she climbed over it, using both hands to speed her descent.

There. She could see them. Brady hovered at the edge of the water, obviously uncertain about his next move. But Brett already had one shoe off.

"Hey!" Olivia shouted, waving her hands. Brady

saw her, smiled and waved back. Brett was wading in. "No!"

But in the next moment Brett tumbled face-first into the swiftly moving water. When it looked like Brady would go in after him, Olivia threw caution aside and raced downhill, ignoring the stabs and jabs of anything that tried to impede her progress.

Brady teetered on one leg, about to lose his balance. Olivia plucked him up and sat him on a big rock several feet from the water's edge.

"Don't you dare move," she ordered. "I can't see Brett."

Big, fat tears tumbled down chubby cheeks. Brady pointed.

"There." He sniffed. "He's not swimming."

Brett lay facedown in the water, floating farther away.

"I'll get him, Brady, but don't you move. Promise me."

"'Kay."

"Good boy." Olivia stepped into the stream. Moving as swiftly as possible, she kept going, though the water was icy cold against her warm skin. In seconds her thin dress was soaked and she was chilled.

Olivia ignored it as she'd learned to ignore the pain of loss that so often gripped her heart. When she was deep enough, she began swimming. It seemed to take forever, but finally she was able to grab a corner of Brett's white tuxedo and tug him into her arms.

Moving as fast as she dared over the sharp yet slippery rocks, Olivia carried the still body to shore. She laid Brett flat and began lifesaving maneuvers she'd learned years ago in a Red Cross class. While she worked, she prayed, vaguely aware that Brady was bawling at the top of his lungs. At least he hadn't moved.

Neither had Brett.

Olivia kept working. Finally the boy responded, spewing a mouthful of water all over her before he gasped for oxygen.

"Thank you, Father," she whispered, holding him as the last of the water gurgled out and his breathing grew more normal.

"No, thank you." Reese grabbed his son's shoulders and helped him sit up. When Brett tried to stand, Reese wrapped him in his arms and held on, eyes squeezed shut. His chest heaved with the exertion of running downhill. Beads of sweat dotted his forehead. His gray-white face looked like an ice sculpture as he hugged the shivering little body against him.

Olivia stayed silent for a few minutes, but finally she touched the shoulder of the man who'd played best man to her bridesmaid in his sister's wedding. His eyes flew open and he stared at her as if awakening from a nightmare.

"Come on, we need to get away from here."

"Yeah. I know." His voice grated, frosted with fear.

Olivia understood that horrible choking awareness that a child you'd protected and adored since birth, a child you would sacrifice your very life for, had almost been snatched away.

Only in her case, there was no almost.

"I'm cold, Daddy," Brett stuttered, his teeth chattering.

"The water comes from snow on the mountains." The leashed tension in Reese's voice chastened the young miscreant into silence as he carried the boy to safety.

Olivia followed them, picking her way back along the water's edge. Her feet screamed a protest, but she ignored it, smiling when Brady blubbered with joy at the sight of his bedraggled twin.

"He's fine, Brady." She led them to a massive boulder that felt deliciously warm to the touch. "Reese?"

"Yeah?" He looked at her, his blue eyes dark as storm clouds.

"He can sit down here." She touched the rock, but Reese didn't move. His arms remained locked around his child. "Brett's cold, Reese. We have to warm him up."

The frantic father studied her for a moment before he looked down at the boy he held. He seemed unable to let go.

"Brett is all right, Reese. But he's cold and wet and we need to fix that." She didn't want to frighten Brett, but his shivering bothered her. She stood on tiptoe and whispered in Reese's ear. "You're scaring him. Put him down, okay?"

He looked at her as if she'd asked him to move mountains.

"Put him down, Reese. I only want to help."

He finally nodded, loosening his grip by degrees until at last Brett had been lowered to the big rock she'd indicated. But Reese remained close by, obviously not quite trusting her with his precious child.

Olivia's heart ached to comfort him some other way, but she was only his wedding partner. So she smiled, then began removing Brett's shirt and pants.

"Come on, sweetheart. Slip out of these wet things. We'll let that big old sun warm you up." When she fumbled, Reese helped, but his stiff, jerky actions gave away his distress.

After a moment, Reese moved toward Brady. His hand shook as he reached for the boy's fingers and a strangled breath squeezed out from his throat at the contact.

"Brady's fine, Reese. Everything is all right now," Olivia soothed softly, hoping to reassure all of them. As she brushed damp brown curls off Brett's forehead, she couldn't resist pressing a kiss against his sweet cheek. "Feeling better, sweetheart?"

"K-kind of." He stared up at her, his spiky lashes stuck together. "Are you going to take off your dress? It's wet, t-too?"

"I'm fine." She suppressed a shiver. "Brady, slip off your jacket, will you? Brett needs it to warm up."

Once Olivia had Brett buttoned inside the white jacket, she gave way to her own weakness and sank down beside him, smothering a groan at the sweet heat of the stone against her skin. Still Reese hovered, silent and grim, holding Brady close.

"It's okay," she repeated softly. "It's okay."

Several minutes passed before Reese nodded. He drew an audible breath, then sat Brady next to Brett. He cupped his palm around each miniature chin, forcing his sons to look at him.

"What were you doing, Brett? Uncle Cade told you not to come down here."

"Y-yes. But I wanted to catch a fish. I almost d-did, too," he chattered, his chin thrusting out with pride.

Olivia's heart lurched at the thought of what might have been. Anika had been four when—

"Uncle Cade said we shouldn't go past those blue flowers." Brady pointed uphill to blooms that were at least three hundred feet above them. "You said that was the rule, didn't you, Daddy?"

Olivia struggled to control her shivering. If only she had enough strength to drag herself back up the hill. But the truth was, she felt drained. Death had come too close.

But it had not taken another child…this time.

"Why did you disobey me and your uncle?" Reese demanded in a rasping voice.

"I don't like rules," Brett said as if that explained everything.

"Too bad. Everybody has to follow rules, Brett." There was no give in Reese's tone. "That's the way life is. Rules help protect us from bad things."

"They didn't pro-teck my mom." Brady mourned. "I heard Great Granny say my mom followed the rules when she stopped at the sign. But my mom got dead." His bottom lip trembled as he glared at his father. "Dead means she's gone, and she isn't coming back ever again."

Reese's mouth worked, but he said nothing. So Olivia took over.

"Do you remember your mother, Brady?"

From her many conversations with Sara, Olivia knew Reese's wife had died several years earlier. The twins would probably not remember her, but Olivia knew it would be helpful to encourage them to talk about her anyway. Maybe something today had triggered a sense of loss.

"Brady doesn't remember nothing."

"Do so. She had brown hair." Brady glared at his brother. "Like choc-lat."

"You saw that in a picture. You don't remember it." Brett's voice wobbled. "I think I do sometimes, but—" He shrugged, his little face confused.

Olivia glanced at Reese, expecting him to soothe them. But he was still dealing with his own shock. His stare remained frozen on the children.

"Sweetheart, your mom is tucked inside here." Olivia tapped Brett's little chest. "She wouldn't care if you remembered what she looked like. All she'd care about is that you remember that she loved you very much."

Brett studied her for a few minutes.

"There's only Daddy and us in our house. It's not like the kids at day care. Most of them have daddies and mommies. I wish I had a mommy."

"Why do you wish that, Brett?" Years of training and thousands of phone calls to a kids' radio show Olivia had taken from a small New York station to national syndication had taught her that talking was often the best therapy.

"The other kids' mommies send cookies on special days and push them on the swings and help say prayers at night." Brady, not Brett, volunteered the information.

"But your dad does things with you, too, doesn't he?"

Please don't let me be wrong.

"Not cookies," Brady corrected. "He does other things."

"The minister at church said God made families with moms and dads." Brett blinked at her through the hank of dark brown hair that flopped over one eye. "We don't gots a mom."

Implying God didn't make his family?

Realizing Reese wasn't capable of responding at that moment, Olivia hurried to reassure.

"God loves all kinds of families, Brett. He loves families with lots of kids and families with only one little boy or girl. He loves families with only a daddy or only a mommy, too. That part doesn't matter to God. What matters is that families love each other. I know you love your daddy."

"Yep," Brett squealed, jumped up. "I love you, Daddy."

"I love you, too." Reese's voice emerged hoarse, choked as he swung his son into his arms and hugged him close. He smiled at Olivia, but it was a distracted courtesy. His attention returned to Brett.

"Why did you come here?" The question held a warning.

Brett's bottom lip jutted out. "To fish."

"What did Cade say?" Reese squatted with Brady resting on his knee. "What did I say, Brett?" His voice was stern, his gaze intense, but his hand, as he lifted it to drag through his hair, trembled. When the boy didn't speak, Reese repeated, "What did I say?"

"Not to."

"What did you promise? Both of you?"

"Not to come." Brady looked at his brother. "I told him not to."

"But you came along with him. After you'd both promised me."

Olivia admired the way Reese forced them to admit their wrongdoing without raising his voice. Though his olive-tanned skin had sallowed and his rich blue eyes still looked haunted by the near disaster, he was trying to teach them.

"I make rules to protect you guys, so you won't get hurt. I do that because I love you and because I don't want anything bad to happen to you." Reese inhaled to steady his voice. "Brett could have drowned. This water is dangerous. It's not a place for kids to come by themselves. Cade told you and I told you, but you disobeyed anyway."

"If I had swimming lessons I could—"

"Brett!"

The little boy gulped, raised his head and looked at his dad, shame washing over his face.

"I'm sorry, Daddy."

"Me, too," Brady chirped right before he wrapped his chubby arms around Reese's neck and squeezed.

Olivia's heart tightened. If only she could feel Anika's beloved arms once more. If only Trevor… Her heart wept as she sent a prayer for peace heavenward.

"I'm sorry, too." Reese sat the boys back down, his tone firmer now. "But being sorry isn't always enough. It wouldn't do any good to be sorry if Brady didn't have a brother anymore, would it, Brett?"

The twins stared at each other as if they'd never imagined such a thing.

"Obedience is important. The only way I can do my daddy job properly is to keep you two safe. That's why you have to obey me."

Fatherhood equaled safety? Olivia frowned.

Reese looked in control, but she saw signs that his emotions were still riding high. And little wonder.

"Do you understand?"

Two brown heads slowly nodded.

"Are we getting punished?"

"Yes, Brett, you are. After Auntie Sara's party, when we're at home. Right now I want you to put on your shoes, take your brother's hand and get back up the hill. Your backpacks are in the house. You can change clothes. Emily will help you." He pointed to the teenage girl who stood at the crest of the hill, watching. "Understand?"

"Yes, Daddy."

They began gathering their belongings.

"Boys?"

They turned, studied Reese with question marks in their eyes.

"Do you have something to say to Olivia?"

"Thank you for helping my brother," Brady said. He gave her a shy hug.

"Yeah. Thanks." Brett offered his hand. Once she'd shaken it, he backed away. "I'm sorry you got wet and your dress got wrecked."

"I'm glad you're okay, Brett."

"No more disobeying," Reese ordered. "You either behave yourselves or we'll go home right now."

"And miss seeing the horsies?" Brady's eyes swelled.

"And miss seeing them," Reese confirmed.

"Come on, Brett." Brady shoved his brother's shoes at him, then nudged him upward. "We gotta be good."

Olivia smiled as she watched the adorable pair scurry uphill. Then her attention returned to Reese.

"Are you all right?"

"I'm not sure I'll ever be all right again," he muttered half under his breath. Then he shook his head at her, smiled. "I'm fine. I lost about five years when I saw you dragging him out. He could have drowned."

"But he didn't. They're all right, thank the Lord."

"The Lord. Yeah." Reese didn't sound as if he was giving God any of the credit for the twins' safety as he tracked their progress uphill.

"They really are all right," Olivia whispered.

"Yeah. I know." But he didn't look away until the young girl, Emily, had them by the hand.

Olivia tried to hide the shiver that rippled over her, but Reese's moody gaze had registered her discomfort.

"I'm sorry. I should have done this earlier." He slid out of his tuxedo jacket and draped it over her shoulders. "Better?"

"Thanks." She sighed as his warmth caressed her goose-pimpled skin.

"It's I who should thank you. When I saw Brett floating on that water, I thought my heart would stop. I couldn't have wished for a better rescuer." His hands fisted at his sides, but when Reese noticed her glance he shoved them in his pockets. "You know your first aid."

"I took a course—the basics, nothing extra. It came in handy."

"Yeah." A half smile lifted his lips. "Thank you."

"You're welcome." She strove for levity to break

the tension. "You didn't step on my bouquet on your way down, did you?"

"Ha! Very funny." His broad white-covered shoulders lifted with his sigh. "What a day."

"A wedding here, a swim there." Olivia shrugged. "Pretty ordinary."

"I'd like to know what kind of life you lead."

"A boring one," she said quickly before he could ask more.

"You have a great rapport with my sons. Of course, Sara told me that when the boys were in that theater project of yours. I must have blocked it."

"Ah." Blocked it or didn't notice?

"Life with those two—" he raked a hand through his hair before jerking a thumb over one shoulder "—doesn't allow a lot of time for thinking. I'm always in protect or prevent mode. They're so little and I couldn't bear it if—"

"I understand." Too well. Losing a child was the nightmare every parent feared most, the thing she'd never thought she'd live through.

Olivia's admiration for Reese grew. Sara's comments about her overprotective brother had painted a very different picture of the man who now looked shaken and disturbed by the incident that had just occurred.

Reese Woodward was actually quite charming.

"We should go." He glanced at her feet. "Your feet must feel horrible. And you seem to have lost your shoes."

"No. I kicked them off before I went in the water. There." She pointed to the edge where her dyed satin slippers looked a lot worse for their trek downhill.

Reese walked over, picked them up and let them dangle from his fingers, chagrin tipping down his wide, generous mouth as he studied her.

"My kids are murder on your wardrobe."

"Yes, but on the bright side," she said after a glance at her bedraggled dress, "at least the wedding pictures have been taken. And it's not like I'm going to wear these clothes again. They have served their purpose. We got Sara and Cade married."

"Yes, we did." He laughed. The sound of relief echoed down the riverbed, a deep-throated burst of pure relief. "Tough lady. I like that. Let's go see if my sister has something you can wear." He bent down, slid the slippers on her feet, then rose and held out a hand.

Olivia took it, allowing him to pull her upright. She held on, borrowing his strength as he helped her climb past the rougher spots, enjoying the sensation of being supported. It had been so long since she'd felt protected, cared for.

"We probably should have gotten to know each other better earlier, but I was trying to make sure a certain pair of ring bearers didn't mess up the whole wedding." He grimaced. "This is really bad timing, but I have been meaning to talk to you about something for the past week and never had the chance."

"Oh?" A tiny coil of fear wound tight inside.

The past was always there, waiting to snag her back into that misery.

"You're a child psychologist."

"Yes, I am." Relief washed through her at the simplicity of that. "But please don't ask me to explain why they decided to go fishing today." She hoped humor would ease his tension while redirecting his questions. "I don't understand the lure of fishing at the best of times."

"Believe me, I intend to find that out firsthand." His lips pinched tightly.

His parenting style wasn't her business, and she was probably overstepping the boundary of a bridesmaid to a best man, but— "Reese?"

"Yeah?" He stared at her, brows lowered. They'd gained the top of the rise and his attention honed in on the twins up ahead, laughing and playing as carefree as if nothing untoward had happened.

"I know they scared the daylights out of you this afternoon, but could you try not to let them see that?"

"Why not?" Reese demanded, his prominent cheekbones jutting sharply in the sunlight. "The twins should know their actions affect others."

"You must teach them that, of course. But maybe not today."

"Because?"

"Because they don't realize how worried you were." She saw his brow furrow and rushed to explain. "That's a good thing, Reese. You don't want to make them afraid of life. You don't want them fussing about all the things that could have happened."

"Brett already has nightmares," he admitted, watching them. "And that talk about their mother— I never even imagined they'd been thinking about her."

"Kids are funny that way. Sometimes they take forever to blurt out what's on their minds," Olivia said. "I'm not trying to tell you how to parent your sons, believe me. I'm just suggesting you might want to focus on the disobedience part of the experience."

Reese studied her for a long time before he exhaled his pent-up breath. He bent his head to one side, then the other as if releasing his tension. Then he nodded.

"Thank you. Again. I needed that reminder."

"You're a good parent. The twins love you and you love them. That's what matters." She changed the subject. "Sara said you work at Weddings by Wood-wards—legal counsel?"

"That's better than the other names she used to call me." He smiled good-naturedly. "I do work as legal counsel for the business, but I also serve on the board at the Byways Youth Center."

"I've heard about it from Sara and some friends. Sounds like it has great potential."

"If we could find a new director." Reese grimaced. "We've been running shorthanded for a while."

"I see."

"Maybe it's something you'd be interested in."

Olivia changed the subject.

"The bridal couple is leaving. I don't want to call Sara back and ruin everything. Maybe I should go home."

"No." Reese frowned as he pulled open the door. "Cade's sister, Karen, will help us. You wait inside. I'll go find her."

He was as good as his word, returning a few minutes later with Karen, who didn't ask any questions, but quickly provided a pale blue sundress and sandals, all the perfect size. Olivia showered, tied her hair back and dressed, feeling almost warm again as she stepped outside.

Reese leaned against the doorpost, watching the twins pet a pony. Brett now wore shorts and a T-shirt. The teenage girl stood beside Reese, talking to him.

"Thanks for lending me this. It's still a bit damp." Olivia handed him his jacket.

"We'll let it hang here to dry," he said, carelessly dropping the expensive jacket over the banister. "Olivia, this is Emily Kirsch. She babysits the twins for me sometimes. Emily, this is Olivia Hastings."

"Nice to meet you. Thank you so much for getting Brett out of the water." Emily clung to her hand, shaking it over and over. "I should have been watching more closely. I don't know what would have happened if you hadn't been there." The girl risked a sideways glance at Reese. "It's all my fault."

"No, it isn't. It's harder to care for the twins here than at home. I know that. I also know you'll watch

them more carefully next time. You did fine, Em."
Reese patted her shoulder, smiled. "You're the best
babysitter they ever had. They love having you care for
them."

"I love them, too. Uh-oh." Emily clapped a hand
over her mouth as Brett tried to get the pony to eat
the ball he was offering. "I better get them busy on
a game. Nice to meet you, Miss Hastings."

Miss. It still sounded strange to hear that.

"You, too," Olivia said, but Emily had already left.
"I'm surprised you remembered my name," she
teased Reese, remembering how he'd stumbled
during an introduction earlier in the day.

He was good-looking in a dangerously rumpled
kind of way. His profile reminded her of Prince
William. One of the twins had left a grubby print on
his shirtfront. The dab of red on his collar matched
the red stain on Brady's white pants. Reese's sandy-
brown hair was just an inch too long to be neat.

"Of course I remember your name." He blinked
innocently.

"You didn't earlier."

"Well, we've already established I was focused on
two small troublemakers. So my brain was occupied
elsewhere." He made a face when Brett began
climbing up a tree and moved forward as if to stop
him. He relaxed when Emily intervened. "If you had
kids, you'd understand how easy it is to get side-
tracked."

If she had kids—

I was a wife and a mother once, her heart cried out. *Until my family was stolen from me.*

"What would you say to a hot cup of coffee and some wedding cake? Emily seems to think those two need their bellies filled. Again."

"Someone actually cut that gorgeous cake?" Olivia walked beside him with the twins following.

His family greeted him with good-natured jeers and teasing. Reese responded in kind, though his attention never left the twins for more than a few minutes.

What would it be like to be part of a family again, to work with kids again, to find the connection that would make her part of something? Olivia longed to join humanity and replace the ever-present worry that held her back, prevented her from getting too close—lest some newspaper reporter figure out whom she'd been and run another story about her pitiful past.

Sara Woodward had been the first person Olivia had trusted in a very long time. And even Sara didn't know the whole truth.

The jury was still out on trusting Reese.

Chapter Two

Two weeks later, Reese could only hope Olivia's interest in touring Byways was genuine enough that she'd cut him some slack for being late for this meeting.

He'd done everything he could to interest her in the director's position, from forwarding reams of accolades for past successes to ideas and possibilities that had been tossed around for the future. As chairman of the board of Byways, he wanted the place to live up to its potential of a refuge where kids could learn new things, find someone to talk to and have a safe place to hang out. Byways needed a director who could oversee everything and deal with questions the kids inevitably needed answers to.

Olivia had remained steadfastly noncommittal—until today when she'd finally agreed to tour the facility with him. Reese sincerely hoped she'd be impressed enough to agree to take the job as director, and soon. Lately he spent almost as much time here as at work, and the twins were not happy about his frequent absences.

Only Nelson's car sat on the lot.

Olivia had given up and gone home and Reese didn't blame her. He was half an hour late. This would have to be the day the twins' nanny quit. He'd been stuck interviewing new candidates all afternoon. The last applicant had scared even him.

Good thing Granny Winnie wasn't above a spot of babysitting when the need arose. If only the twins didn't—

"You think *I* should work here, but *you're* afraid to get out of your own car? Is that your excuse for being late?"

Reese snapped out of his reverie to see Olivia laughing down at him. She looked different today. Not because she was less elegant in her navy slacks and sleeveless white shirt with a navy jacket slung over one arm. It was her hair that caught his attention. Again.

It was as lovely as he remembered. Loose, flowing to her shoulders in a swath of blended honey and amber, it glistened with a hint of orange—no, cinnamon—enhancing the flawless perfection of her face.

"I like your hair," he blurted out.

"Oh. Well. Thank you." Olivia's smile faltered as she lifted a hand to brush the long spiky bangs off her forehead.

Idiot!

Reese chided himself for embarrassing her as he climbed out of his car. Too bad he hadn't concentrated on what he intended to say instead of her hair.

"So. Should we risk it and go inside?"

Her lighthearted comment killed his tension.

"Yes." Reese locked his car then began telling the history of Byways. "An elderly man used to live here, a grouch who put up a big fence around the place to keep the neighborhood kids out. But his yard was the perfect place to play catch and the kids always found a way in. He began sitting at the window, watching them play. The laughter and voices cheered him up and he soon looked forward to their coming."

"Charming, but is it true?"

"Oh, yes. So Mr. Mung changed from the old grouch he'd been. But suddenly the kids stopped coming. He couldn't figure out why, but he knew he wanted them to come back. He missed the way they made him feel younger."

"Why did they stop?" She matched her step to his.

"Some do-gooder built them a softball field." Reese chuckled at her droll look. "Mung figured that if he took his broken fence down, the kids might come back. He was trying to remove it when one of the kids passed, a punk who had been troubling the neighborhood for years. They argued. Short version is Mung had a heart attack, the kid got him to hospital and while Mung was away, the kid and his punk friends took down the wrecked fence, mowed the yard and started meeting on the front lawn."

"Nice."

"They say guilt is a great motivator. Anyway, when he came home, Mung couldn't keep up the yard without help. The kid noticed, got his friends to pitch in and pretty soon Mung's place became their drop-in center. The kids began to tell him their stories and Mung showed them a new perspective. When he couldn't help, he conned his neighbor, a counselor, into stopping by. The word spread."

Reese paused to catch his breath, but Olivia was way ahead of him.

"So Mung left the kid the house, the kid called it Byways and found funding to keep it running as a youth center." Olivia slid her fingers over the worn sign that sat at the bottom of the stairs. "That kid was you. I do love a happy ending."

Reese studied her more intensely.

"You've been doing your homework, Miss Hastings."

"I like to know what I'm getting into, Mr. Woodward." She tossed him a cheeky grin then skipped up the stairs.

"And?" Reese followed, wondering where this was leading.

"I've done some checking. Byways has a great reputation as a safe place where kids can come to have fun, share and, with a little help, figure themselves out. So far I'm quite intrigued by this place."

"Intrigued is good." Reese followed her inside, trying to quell his fervent hope that she'd agree to take on the directorship and give him, its chairman, a breather.

A tall, lean man met them in the foyer.

"Olivia Hastings, this is Nelson Kirsch, Emily's brother. Nelson is our activities director. Nelson, Miss Hastings is considering joining Byways."

"Joining as what?" Nelson lifted one eyebrow in his inimitably imperious way.

Irritation pricked Reese at Nelson's snarky tone, though he knew the reason for it. Nelson wanted to be offered the job as director, though he didn't have the necessary credentials. But before Reese could say anything, Olivia thrust out her hand.

"As whatever I can be to help, Mr. Kirsch." She waited for him shake. "I hope that won't be a problem."

"That remains to be seen, Miss Hastings." Nelson shook her hand once, then quickly dropped it. "Excuse me. I'm putting the last few details in place for a day trip."

"Certainly." Olivia stepped back to allow him to pass. When he'd disappeared, she glanced at Reese. "The temperature seems to have dropped."

"That's just Nelson."

"You mean he thaws out?"

"Truthfully? Not really. Ah, here's Emily. Hi, Em." Reese hugged her thin shoulders and frowned when she immediately tensed, then slipped away. "You okay?"

"Sure. How are the twins? Did Brett get sick from that dunking?"

"His sickness came on after he found out their punishment was to peel potatoes for a week." Reese winked at Olivia. "Brett isn't fond of the job and he gets testy when Brady outdoes him with the plastic peelers I bought. Peeling potatoes keeps them busy and gives both of them time to think about the error of their ways."

"Potatoes." Olivia chuckled. "That's creative."

"Mr. Woodward has lots of ideas." Emily threw him a cheeky grin. "We mess up his house real bad sometimes when I look after the kids. He usually tricks me into helping clean up. But he never gets mad at me."

"Do other people get mad at you, Emily?" Olivia asked softly. Something wasn't quite right with Emily. She could sense it.

"Sometimes." Emily cast a worried look over one shoulder. "I gotta go. We're going fishing."

"Don't eat the worms if you don't catch anything."

"Yuck. That'd be a Brady thing." She slipped out from under Reese's hand as he tried to ruffle her hair and raced away, giggling.

"She's the nicest kid and she's great with the twins."

"I can hear a 'but' in there."

"I don't know how to say it. Lately I sense she's afraid of me. Maybe it's because I'm so much bigger than her." He caught Olivia staring at him. "You're the child psychologist. What do you think?"

"Maybe you're right." Olivia's noncommittal answer left a lot to be desired. She glanced around. "How often do they go on field trips?"

"Almost every day in the summer. Nelson has a schedule of things for them to do. I'm not sure why they need to go out all the time, but Nelson seems to feel it's best and the kids do gain exposure to a lot of activities that they'd miss if they stayed here."

"I hear another 'but.'"

"It's a nightmare getting all the permission slips accounted for. But I won't risk a lawsuit."

"Very wise. They guarantee no parent can claim ignorance."

"That's the plan." Reese led her through the building.

"Not much actually happens here in the center now, though, does it?" Olivia studied the gym area that had become more of a storage room. "That's too bad. It looks like your funding is pretty solid. I've seen colleges with less equipment than this place."

"We have corporate support and a couple of bequests we can tap into for repair or to replace, if necessary. Nelson has about six staff." He looked around, shrugged. "We have at least two on the premises at all times when we're open."

"Smart. But what does the staff do? If there are no events held here, I mean."

"I'm not sure," he admitted, "but Nelson keeps them busy. We used to have lots of things happening at Byways, but not recently. That's something I hope a new director might change."

"Because?"

"As a board, we feel Byways should be the center of activity and not simply a place to catch a bus. Activities are nice, but run properly we could offer more. I feel our staff is under-utilized in the current situation. We have good people who just need some direction and fresh vision." Reese told himself it was okay to feel a little proud of what he'd helped accomplish. "I think our salaries are pretty competitive, too."

He explained the range for the managing director's position.

"Very reasonable, although, for me, the job isn't about the money." Olivia inspected the director's office after he'd unlocked it, glanced at the operating budget. "For me, it's more about the kids and the things Byways offers to help them."

"We are happy to hear any and all suggestions."

The tour over, Reese led her to the kitchen area now used for staff breaks, hoping that light in her eyes had intensified because she was interested.

"Let's take a break. Coffee?" He poured two cups, held one up.

"Black, please."

He indicated she should sit in one of the easy chairs before he handed the cup to her.

"Thanks." Olivia sipped her coffee. Silence stretched between them before she spoke again. "If my opinion counts, I'd say Byways has a very effective board. Everything looks well maintained. I don't understand why this job is still open."

"Frankly, neither do we." Reese hated this part, but he had to be honest. "We've had several applicants accept our offer in the past two years. They each came in, worked for six to nine months and then gave their notice."

"Because?"

He flopped down in the chair across from her, rolled his head from side to side to ease the tension in his neck. "The work isn't what they expected. The job isn't what they want. Like that."

"How many candidates have come and gone?"

"Three, so far."

"None of them stayed even a year?" Olivia blinked, hazel eyes darkening as the gold flecks melted. When he shook his head, her irises dimmed to the shade of forest shadows in the mountains outside Denver. She sipped her coffee, but kept her gaze on him. "Oh."

"Exactly." Reese nodded.

"What happened to your last director?"

"He quit six months ago. Said he wanted a different line of work. There was some, uh, tension in the office. We've had a complete turnover of other staff since then. Except for Nelson, of course. He's been here forever."

"And he applied for the director's job." Olivia rubbed the bridge of her nose with one knuckle.

"You knew?"

"The attitude gives it away."

"I suppose." Why did he always feel he had to apologize for Nelson? "After the last one quit I think Nelson was so sick of the constant changeovers he decided he could do the job himself. But he can't." Reese wanted to make it clear Nelson was not her competition.

"Because?"

"We have to comply with state and city regulations by having a qualified counselor who approves our programs—and Nelson isn't, he simply doesn't have the training to talk someone down, counsel them about the future or offer advice for problems. He's not interested in going back to school, either. So the day trips continue."

Reese thought he could watch her hair forever. The unusual shades seemed to change every time Olivia moved her head. She wasn't the least bit plain or retiring, but she had a way of seeming to melt into the background that encouraged him to lose whatever reticence he might have. Reese wasn't sure if that was a good thing.

"What do you do now?"

"A local psychologist comes in two days a week. She's made it clear it's only temporary and that she'd like to go back to her private practice—yesterday. Kids are not her forte so perhaps it's as well she isn't staying."

Olivia didn't ask any more. She finished her coffee, rose and walked over to read the notices on the bulletin board. She flipped through the canvases Byways's art students had created last winter and checked out the marionettes swaying from the ceiling.

Reese held his tongue, willing to give her all the time she needed to decide. He hoped she'd agree to take the job quickly because he needed to get on the phone and find a new nanny fast.

After many moments had passed, Olivia turned to face him.

"I am a board-certified child psychologist, licensed to practice in Colorado." Olivia listed her degrees and the colleges where she'd attained them, her voice neither boastful nor deferring. She was simply stating her qualifications. "I have not been employed for several years, however, so I don't have any current references."

"Were you ill?" Reese didn't think she looked unhealthy.

"No. Family problems. I am single, I have no dependents. I, er, moved from the East to start again." And she didn't want to talk about it. That much was crystal clear from the solid jut of her chin as she stared at him.

Reese didn't hold it against her. He didn't like to talk about his past, either.

"But you do have experience? References from your past employment?"

"I had my own practice, which is now defunct, but yes, there are people who will vouch for me. Professional and otherwise."

He studied her, confused by the eagerness he'd glimpsed in her eyes and the stiff, unyielding way she held herself, as if she wasn't quite ready to commit.

"Are you applying for the job, Olivia?" he asked quietly when time had elapsed and she hadn't spoken or looked at him again.

She lifted her head, met his stare.

"I'm definitely interested." Her back straightened. "But I do need to pray about it and learn God's will on the matter before I make a final decision."

"Okay." Reese rose, gathered their cups and placed them in the sink.

"But."

"But?" He whirled around unable to keep hope from sneaking into his voice. "What does 'but' mean?"

"I would like to learn more about Byways, about what's worked in the past and what has failed. I want to get the feel of the operation and hear a little more about the board's expectations." Her voice dropped, but her hazel eyes did not avoid his scrutiny. "Mostly I want time to pray about it, make sure Byways is where God wants me to be."

"And then?" he prodded.

"As soon as I'm certain, I'll give you my decision." Her shoulders lifted, her spine straightened. "I don't know why your other applicants quit, Reese, but if I don't take this job, my reason will be because I do not feel this is where God wants me."

"You're a person of strong faith, aren't you?" He didn't need to ask, but Reese did anyway because he wanted Olivia Hastings to talk and he wanted to listen to the smooth soft lilt of her voice. He wanted to see her eyes flash from green to gold again, as they did every time she spoke of God.

Most of all, he wanted to know what situation had brought her to Denver and how God had helped her. Maybe then he'd understand why God never seemed to be there for him or his boys, though the family would be shocked to hear him say that.

"Strong faith?" Olivia raised her eyebrows as she considered the term, then nodded. "Yes, I guess you could say that. I believe in God. I believe I am His child and that He will show me the way I should go, if I pay attention and wait for His leading."

"And do you always do that—wait?"

"Always," she said with a smile. "I've learned it works better that way."

Was that his problem? Reese wondered. Did he not wait long enough for God to show him which way to go? But it had been almost three years since Taylor had been hit by a drunk driver on her way home with a quart of milk.

Couldn't God have gotten in touch once in three years?

Anger bubbled to the surface, but Reese was sick of being angry. It never did any good. He pushed it away, wishing he had the same solid confidence in God as Olivia.

"How long do you need?"

"I'm sorry, but you see that's where the waiting

part comes in. I don't know how long it will take."
She smiled. "If someone else comes along in the
meantime, I'll gladly step out of the way. But I have
to be sure."

"You do realize we'll need to do a background
check in either case? It's policy," he added when she
seemed to freeze for a second.

"Yes, of course. The safety of the children is always
paramount." Olivia recovered quickly and led the
way out of the room. She walked beside him out of
the building. "I'm sure you have things to do. I'll fax
you my information if you'll give me your number."

Reese pulled a card out of his pocket and handed
it to her.

"That's my e-mail address and fax at Weddings by
Woodwards," he explained. "I'm not usually at
Byways every day."

"I'll send you my information soon. I'm sure
you're anxious to get home to the twins." She tucked
the card into her pocket and asked, "How are they?"

"Busy." Reese sighed. "Their nanny quit today.
Brett 'colored' her sandals."

Olivia held her hands up as if to hold him back.
"I'm not even going to ask."

"Thank you for that." He unlocked his car. "You're
parked nearby?"

"My car recently retired. I'm looking into a new
one. I took a cab here."

"You need a ride then." He moved to open the
passenger door, but she stopped him.

"No. I told the driver to come back in—here he is,"

she said as a taxi rolled up beside them. "Thanks for meeting me, Reese. I'm glad I came."

"Great. Thanks a lot, Olivia."

"Thank you. This might be just what I need." With a funny little smile that roused his curiosity, Olivia waggled her fingers then left.

Reese drove toward Weddings by Woodwards and the briefcase of work that needed to be finished before his meeting tomorrow morning. He had yet to hire a nanny. Day care and preschool couldn't begin to cover the hours he worked or the emergencies that sometimes came up.

The parking lot at Weddings by Woodwards lay empty when he pulled into his spot. He'd barely opened the back door when someone called his name. His guard went up automatically. The parking lot was out of the way. No clients came back here.

Frowning, he waited as a young woman he didn't recognize walked toward him.

"Were you calling me?"

"Reese Woodward?"

He nodded. "Yes."

She drew an envelope out of her jacket and held it out.

"I was asked to see that you got this personally, ASAP."

He glanced from the paper to her disappearing figure, surprised.

Using his finger, he slit open the letter and drew out the papers inside. He caught his breath.

Weddings by Woodwards had plans to open a new store in Chicago. Reese had scouted the location, chosen the perfect site on Chicago's famous Magnificent Mile. He'd lobbied the owners for a long-term lease and revised his terms several times. In fact, just yesterday he'd requested more changes to ensure his grandmother's requests for the new store were met on every level.

Apparently he'd hesitated too long.

Dear Mr. Woodward:

I apologize for taking this extreme measure to contact you, but I felt you should know immediately of Mr. Garver's untimely passing this morning. You will understand that the family is extremely emotional at this time, but Mrs. Garver is most insistent that I notify you at the earliest possible date of her intentions. Those intentions include liquidating all her real estate assets, meaning she will put the Chicago property up for sale. Because of the amount of time you and her husband spent discussing a possible lease, and because Mr. Garver thought very highly of you, Mrs. Garver is granting you first offer of sale. I have enclosed the amount and terms she's requesting. You should know that she intends to move to be nearer her daughter in France as soon as can be arranged, and thus wishes to close the sale on the prop-

*erty this month. I would be most appreciative if
you could let me know your decision as soon as
possible…*

Reese's breath whooshed out of him as if someone
had plunged a fist into his solar plexus.

His family was counting on a smooth transition.
He'd reassured his grandmother only this morning
that he would get everything she'd requested, that
there would be no problems with this property, that
he'd chosen the best possible building. Because of
him, they hadn't even looked at other possibilities,
content to let him nitpick over every detail because
they trusted him.

If only he'd stopped haggling and agreed to sign
the lease sooner!

There was no way they could buy the property.
Renovations on the Denver store had exceeded their
budget. A tripling in costs of organza and silk had
affected Winifred's latest collection and their bottom
line because the pricing had been preset for the cat-
alogues. If that weren't enough, a fire in the sewing
factory two months ago had taken its toll on
Weddings by Woodwards' bank account.

Yet time after time Reese had reassured each
family member that he had everything in Chicago
well in hand. How stupid they'd been to trust him.

His grandmother's favorite phrase echoed in his
head.

God's in His Heaven, all's right with the world.
Well, where was God now?

Chapter Three

Olivia loved the first pink rays of dawn. She especially loved sitting on the patio, hugging a big mug of coffee close as the flamingo fingers of dawn crept over the mountains and colored the sky with promise.

The thought of having a job to go to wasn't bad, either.

She'd been working at Byways for two weeks now, and each time she walked through the door she still felt the same rush of anticipation. She still relished the young faces that came looking for something. She still caught her breath at the possibility of once more sharing something good, fulfilling and satisfying.

"Thanks for being the God of second chances," Olivia whispered, her heart overflowing.

She was certain now that Byways was where God wanted her. In truth, she'd known it the day she'd toured the place with Reese. But she'd waited; both for the rock-solid certainty that now nestled inside her heart and the latest report from her friend, Nancy, to be certain that no one was nosing around the last place she'd lived, asking for an interview, demanding to know how her tragic life had moved on.

She picked up the phone on its first ring.

"Did I wake you?" Nancy sounded out of breath.

"No. I've been sitting here watching the sunrise." Her fingers squeezed around the phone nervously. "Is anything wrong?"

"No. But I have information I thought you should know. Olivia, two reporters have been digging into your past. One contacted me. Apparently, he's doing an anniversary story on Anika and Trevor. You know the kind of thing—three years ago today…" She stopped, unwilling to repeat the horrible tragedy aloud.

"Okay. Do they know where I am?"

"No, I'm pretty sure not. I just wanted you to be aware."

"Thanks, Nancy. You're the best friend I've ever had. I'm sorry this has put you out so much."

"I'm at my favorite coffee shop talking to my best friend. No problem." Her voice softened. "How are you?"

"I'm healing. I've found a job I love and it's mostly perfect."

"Mostly?"

"Well, there is this thorn in my side named Nelson.

But I'm coping." They chatted for several more minutes, catching up on each other's lives. Then Nancy had to go. "Is there a number where I could reach you at Byways in case something else comes up?"

Olivia hesitated, but finally recited the number. "Remember, I'm Olivia Hastings now."

"Take care of yourself, sweetie. Keep trusting God."

"I am. Thanks for calling." Olivia hung up before she allowed the tears to fall.

One splashed against the photo propped in her lap. Anika and Nancy's daughter Cara had played together like sisters. Trevor and Nancy's husband had been high school buddies. Everything had been so perfect.

"I miss you, darlings," she whispered, tracing one fingertip over the ruggedly handsome face of the only man she'd ever loved. "You were the best part of me, Trevor. You kept me focused on the important things. I know you're glad I'm at Byways."

A little girl with a gap-toothed smile and hair the exact shade of Olivia's snuggled on her daddy's knee, beaming. Olivia couldn't stop the tear that tumbled down her cheek, even though she knew these precious ones were beyond hurt and pain, in a place where love lived.

"Be happy, baby. Look after Daddy, okay?" Olivia carried the photo inside, set it on her mantle. They were at peace now. And she was slowly finding serenity for herself. At last Olivia felt ready to move ahead with her life.

But to truly move ahead, she needed to put down roots. The condo was nice, but it came furnished. There was nothing of Olivia in it. Maybe this weekend she'd contact a real estate agent to initiate her search for a place to begin again.

Olivia dressed carefully, wondering what negative remark Nelson would find to object to her plans today. Not that he would be loud and obnoxious. He wasn't. Nelson was more like a toothache. Annoying, painful and always there, pressing on your last nerve.

Still, it wasn't the first time Olivia had had to work with an unhappy coworker. It wouldn't be the last. It was just that with Nelson, life was trying when it didn't have to be. All Olivia wanted was for Byways to be the most effective youth center in the city. That meant doing away with some of the old ways and adopting a few new ones.

Unfortunately therein lay Nelson's biggest problem. He took affront with every suggestion she offered. Soon she'd be walking on pins and needles to avoid raising his hackles. And that would make her less effective—something that bothered Olivia. A lot.

"Give me strength today, Lord," she prayed as she drove. "Let me be a peacemaker. Most of all, help me meet the kids' needs."

By the time she arrived at Byways, the bloated red sky had altered, now blooming a funny purplish shade. The air hung heavy with the cloying humidity that portended a storm. Hopefully the tempest would only be on the outside of Byways.

"Good morning everyone," she said brightly as she stepped into the office.

Glowering silence greeted her. Not a good sign. Olivia sighed.

"What's wrong?"

"I understand you've canceled today's outing and substituted something else," Nelson said.

"Yes, I did."

"Perhaps you don't understand how things work around here, Olivia." Nelson's icy tones brimmed with patronization. "As activities director, I make the arrangements for events inside and outside this building. You were hired to take care of counseling. You do not override my plans without a good reason."

Oh, brother.

"I do when the chairman of the board asks me to, Nelson," she said quietly. "Since some of the permission slips were not returned, Reese asked me to organize something else. Which I've done. Because you weren't here."

"I was busy managing fifty kids on a field trip!"

"Nor did you answer your cell phone, which is against the rules," she reminded quietly, "or I would have apprised you of the situation ahead of time. As it was, all I could do was to leave you a note."

"Reese asked you?" His eyebrows arched. "You

two are getting pretty tight. Something you want to tell us, Olivia?" His voice sneered her name.

Olivia glanced at her secretary for a hint, but Casey only rolled her eyes. Time to face his antagonism head-on.

"Innuendo doesn't work with me, Nelson. If you have something to say, then say it. Otherwise let's get busy." She waited a moment, pinning him with her best "teacher" look. When he said nothing more, she marched past him to her office.

Casey followed a few seconds later with the mail.

"He's a royal pain—"

"Is everything arranged for the party this afternoon?" Olivia asked, cutting off the diatribe about to spill. The heavy weather outside seemed to seep in and swell the sense of unease filling the building. She didn't want to add to it.

"All taken care of, boss. The kids are gonna love it." Casey prattled on about the events planned for the afternoon. When the phone rang, she grabbed it. "Byways. This is Casey. Oh, sure. Just a sec."

Casey held out the phone.

"For me?"

"Reese Woodward." Casey winked before giving her the receiver. "I'll get back to my desk and head off Nelson if he comes near."

"Thanks, Casey. Hello, Reese. Is everything okay?"

"Hi, Olivia. I had a phone call from another board member. There's been a bad accident a couple of miles from you. Apparently they're going to cut power in your area while they do some extensive repairs. The electrical disruption is expected to last until near dinnertime, which makes this afternoon a no-go."

"That's a shame."

"Yes. I suggest you put up a sign canceling whatever you'd planned in place of Nelson's outing and go home. It's going to storm anyway. Thankfully our area should be okay, which is good because I need some heavy-duty computer time."

"Thanks for the warning. I'll get Casey to put up some signs right away."

"Good." He sounded tired, fed up.

"Reese?"

"Yeah?"

"Is everything okay?" She felt stupid for asking. They were acquaintances. Boss and employee. But she heard a tone in his voice, a tinge of defeat he couldn't quite mask, and it bothered her. "Surely you're not having to race around and find a place for a wedding today? Who gets married on a Monday?"

"You'd be surprised. We actually do about eighteen Monday weddings per year," he said. "But I'm not even at work yet."

"Why not? Kids sick?"

"They're healthy as hogs. No, it's the same old nanny problem and since the day care I use is on your side of the town, it's also shutting down for today. I'm trying to juggle things." He rasped a harsh laugh. "Between filling your job at Byways and trying to keep a nanny, I'm starting to feel like an employment agency."

"I'm sorry." That sounded woefully inadequate.

"Yeah, me, too. But thanks."

"Reese? Would it be okay—I mean, since I have the day off and everything." Olivia paused, squeezed her eyes closed and counted to ten. "What if I took care of the twins today? I have nothing else planned, so it's not a problem."

"Really? You wouldn't mind?"

"I'd love to see the boys again." She meant it. But she also wanted to see him, too.

For some reason Olivia couldn't quite dislodge Reese's face from her mind, though she'd told herself to get over it a thousand times. She was not interested in a romantic relationship and there was a good reason for that. Being the fodder for gossip tabloids meant everyone you came into contact with was a target. Granted, few people outside New York would remember her, but Brett and Brady were totally photogenic. As was their father. Add in the notoriety of Weddings by Woodwards and who knows how big an enterprising reporter could make the story.

Stop worrying. Nancy said no one knows where you are.

Silence gaped across the phone connection like a chasm too wide to cross.

"Reese?" She regretted offering. After all, they

were strangers. She'd only been a bridesmaid in his sister's wedding. "Never mind—"

"If you're really sure, I'll be forever grateful."

"I'm really sure." Funny how sure she was.

"Then thank you." A crash sounded in the background. "Want to change your mind, Olivia?" he murmured.

She laughed.

"No. But I'll need directions how to get there."

Reese told her, then added, "Drive carefully."

Olivia hung up the phone, smiling at the ruckus she'd heard in the background.

"So now you're babysitting his kids." Nelson leaned against the door frame, his face expressing his displeasure.

"I don't think it's polite to listen in on other people's conversations, do you?" Olivia stared at him for a second. Seeing no remorse she gathered her bag and her jacket. "I was about to tell you and Casey that we have to cancel out today. Reese says the power's going to be shut off and will probably stay that way till this evening, so we're to close up shop for the day. I hope that won't put you out too much."

"That's not exactly true, is it, Olivia?" A sneer stretched his lips, marring Nelson's good looks. "You really don't care if my plans are ruined at all."

"You're wrong about that. But I'm not going to argue with you. I'll see you tomorrow." She paused outside her office, waiting for him to leave so she could lock the door.

Nelson made her wait a few seconds before ambling out of the room. He stood watching her, as if memorizing the way she turned the deadbolt and checked to make sure the door was locked.

"Secrets protected, Olivia?"

"I have nothing to hide." *But I don't want my life on the front page anymore.*

"Sure you don't. How come nobody's heard of you?"

"Lots of people have heard of me."

"I heard your references were rather skimpy."

Frustration vied with anger. Olivia fought to keep both from showing and sent a prayer for help heavenward. Composing herself, she slid the handle of her bag over one shoulder and dug her keys from the outside pocket.

Then she looked him squarely in the eye.

"The board was completely satisfied with my references." She exhaled and tried again. "I don't know why you're acting like this, Nelson. I'm not at Byways to ruin your world or make your life difficult. I am here for the children. I intend to do the very best I can for them, for as long as I'm here. And nothing you can say will sway me from that goal."

"Uh-huh."

Olivia paused a fraction of a second longer, maintaining eye contact. Then in her softest voice, "Excuse me."

Nelson stepped back, waved her past.

"Of course. I'll lock the place up for you and make

sure all the other details are seen to while you go off and have your date with the chairman."

It took every ounce of strength Olivia could muster to keep walking. She found Casey, told her the plan, then left. When she finally reached her car, she kept her back to Byways as she drew in deep cleansing breaths.

"I didn't mean to listen to your conversation, Olivia." Emily stood behind her. She danced from one foot to the other. "But I heard what my brother said in the hallway. You're going to Mr. Woodward's."

"Yes." Olivia felt sorry for the thirteen-year-old. Having Nelson for a brother must be difficult. "I'm going to look after the twins for the day. Their nanny quit."

"Can I go with you? Please? I'm used to babysitting them, I could help." Emily tracked Olivia's gaze back to the building where her brother stood on the top step, watching them. "Please? I really want to go." She sounded nervous. "I need to."

Need to? Olivia studied the young girl, saw shadows in her eyes.

"Is anything wrong, Emily?"

"No." It came out too quickly. Emily darted another glance over her shoulder. "I just need to get away from here today," she said, desperation edging her voice. "I promise I won't cause any trouble. I'll do whatever you want me to. But please, let me come."

The look crouching at the back of Emily's eyes reminded Olivia of her own feelings when cameras had been shoved in her face, harassing her, intruding into her grief. All she'd wanted was to escape. Emily's face bore that same fear.

"You've babysat the twins before. Maybe you should go instead of me," Olivia murmured, stalling for time. Nelson was still watching them.

"I—I don't want to babysit all alone. I'm kind of—tired." Emily's jerky voice came out in little gasps. "I was up late last night."

"How come?" Olivia didn't understand why the girl wanted to escape, but she recognized the extreme anxiety in Emily's voice. The way she kept checking to see if her brother was still watching them was curious. It wasn't that Olivia wouldn't welcome the extra help with the two busy boys, but she had a feeling allowing Emily to come with her would only irritate Nelson more and she did not need that. "Were you sick?"

"No." Emily blurted the word out too fast. "I was busy doing—stuff. It took longer than I figured. You could phone Mr. Woodward and see if it's all right, couldn't you?" Emily's big eyes implored her to say yes. "I wouldn't be any problem. I promise."

"I'm not worried about that, honey." Instinct was telling Olivia that Emily had come to her for help. She didn't know why yet, but she did know she could not fail the girl. "Look, I'll call Reese and get his approval while you check with your brother. I have to have Nelson's permission to take you with me."

After a long pause, Emily agreed. As she slowly walked across the parking lot, Olivia pulled out her cell phone and explained the situation to Reese. He sounded puzzled.

"So I get two babysitters. The twins are going to be ecstatic. They've been talking about you constantly." He chuckled. "Of course Emily can come. In fact, if she wants, she can babysit on her own. I've been trying not to ask her because I know she loves being with the other kids at Byways and babysitting full-time is no way for a thirteen-year-old to spend her summer."

"She loves Byways, but she adores the twins." At Byways, Emily was also with Nelson most of the time, and Olivia was no longer certain that was a good thing.

"Hey, if she comes today, you'd be free to do other things."

"I suggested that, but she said she was too tired to babysit on her own. I think something's wrong between her and Nelson, though I'm not sure what that might be." Olivia reassured him she'd do her best to find out the problem. "Maybe she'll relax with the twins and tell me what's wrong."

"Maybe. They probably had an argument."

"I think it's more than that."

"Such as?"

"I don't know. Yet." She changed the subject. "Are you trying to do me out of a day with those two sweethearts, Reese?"

"No way. If you're sure, come on over and bring Emily. She can probably use a break."

"I'm sure. We'll see you in a bit." Olivia snapped the phone shut.

Her gaze slid to brother and sister, who stood facing each other on the stairs. She couldn't hear what Nelson was saying, but Olivia could see the effect it was having on Emily. Her whole body sagged as if she'd been physically hit. Her chin dropped to her chest, her pretty face lost all animation as she stared at the ground.

Olivia fumed. Nelson could be as miserable to her as he wanted, but he was not going to take it out on his sister if she could help it. She tossed her handbag in the car, slammed the door and started forward.

"Is there a problem with Emily coming with me, Nelson?" she called. "I'll be responsible for her."

For a moment it looked as if Nelson would argue. But then he said something to Emily, some whispered remark that Olivia couldn't hear. Emily backed away, but she nodded quickly, obviously agreeing to whatever he stipulated.

"Fine. Emily can go. But I expect her at home by seven. No later."

"Not a problem. Thanks, Nelson." Olivia grabbed Emily's hand, found it icy cold. "Come on, Em. Let's blow this place," she said, and pulled her toward the car.

"I've never heard you talk like that." Emily clambered into the car. The relief on her face did not need translating.

"You're going to hear lots of stuff today. I've never babysat twins before." Olivia switched on the engine and shifted into gear. "Hang on to your hat. Time to get to work at the Woodward house."

The Kirsch siblings' relationship had bothered Olivia ever since she'd come to Byways. Now a niggling worry would not be silenced. Something was clearly wrong between Emily and Nelson. Olivia needed to find out what.

"Mr. Woodward said it was all right for me to come?"

"Of course. Why wouldn't he want you to come over?" She glanced sideways, but Emily would not meet her gaze.

"I thought maybe since the boys got in the water at the wedding, that Mr. Woodward wouldn't want me around them so much." Emily turned to stare out the window.

"I'm sure you're wrong about that. Reese told me you're great with the twins. He wouldn't lie about that and if he didn't want you with them, he wouldn't have said you could come today. He sure wouldn't have enough faith in you to try to send me home."

"Send you home?"

"He thought you'd be okay to babysit by yourself. That doesn't sound like he blames you for anything. Does it?"

"I guess not." Something was definitely wrong.

"Emily, you know that if you ever need to talk to someone, about anything, I will always listen, don't you?"

Emily kept staring out the window. A moment later she reached up to scrub her knuckles against her cheek.

"Thanks," she whispered.

Olivia's misgivings grew. But she said no more, leaving it to Emily to initiate conversation when she was ready. A few minutes later the girl relaxed enough to point out interesting things along the way. Soon she was chatting freely, and by the time they arrived at Reese's house, she seemed perfectly comfortable.

"I am so glad to see you. Both of you."

Olivia didn't think the look on Reese's face was relief, but she couldn't quite decipher what it was, other than to say it made her heart rate increase and her skin feel warm.

Though he was dressed in his usual business attire, Reese did not look as polished as usual. His sandy hair stood up in unruly tufts. There was a green streak marring the perfection of his pristine white shirt-front—marker perhaps?—and evidence of white hand prints on his knee. A splotch of red decorated the underside of his jaw.

The twins raced outside and enveloped them in jubilant hugs. Olivia hugged them back, genuinely glad to see the children again.

"Can we go jump on the trampoline, Mr. Woodward?"

Emily had each child by the hand, holding them back as they strained to pull her inside the house.

"Sure." Reese nodded. "Sure. But make sure the netting is fastened around the side."

"I always do." Her giggles burst out as the twins pulled hard on her arms. "I'm coming, Brett. I'm coming!"

"Hold on a second, guys. Don't I get a hug before I go?"

Olivia's heart gave a bump of longing as Reese's big strong arms gathered his sons' wriggling bodies to his chest. Her arms ached to hold her own child again, to feel the bliss of baby-soft skin against hers, to breathe the sweaty aroma of a busy child on a warm day, to hear a certain voice chirp, "I love you, Mama."

"Olivia?"

She blinked away the mist of the past and found she was alone with Reese.

"Sorry." Her mocking half-laugh sounded shaky in her own ears. "Guess I zoned out. Any last-minute directions?"

"More like warnings. Tons of them." His eyes held hers, a question in their depths. "But I haven't got time right now." He rasped a hand across his jaw. "I didn't even have time to shave this morning."

"I believe that stubbled look is very fashionable." The way he kept watching her told Olivia something else was going on. "There's nothing wrong, is there?"

"What's with Emily?"

"I don't know yet. She asked, no make that *begged*, to come." Ordinarily Olivia wouldn't have shared her concerns, but as Nelson worked for Byways, and since Reese was head of the board, she felt it important to go on the record with her suspicions. "I think she and Nelson were arguing about something. Their relationship troubles me."

"Because?" He frowned.

"It's too early to be certain and I'd just be voicing suspicions, but next time you're at Byways, watch their interaction. I'll be interested in your opinion."

"I'm not sure my opinion is worth much lately," Reese muttered.

"Want to explain that?" It wasn't only her emotional reaction to him. Olivia knew something else was going on with him.

"Not right now." He dragged a hand through his hair. "I've got to get to work. I'm sorry to dump this on you and run. It's a lot to ask."

"It's fine. Besides, I have Emily to help me."

"Yeah." His cell phone rang. "Yes, Grandmother. I realize I have two clients waiting. I got hung up, but I'm on my way now. Thanks."

She saw the way Reese glanced wistfully toward the house as the children's laughter carried toward them.

"They'll be fine," she said softly.

"I know. Thanks." He turned toward his car.

"Wait!" Olivia grabbed his arm then dropped her

hand when he turned to stare at her. "Sorry, but there's this little problem. May I?"

Reese said nothing, simply inclined his head, granting permission. She moved in front of him, lifted her hand and touched the rock-solid edge of his jaw.

"Is this blob of ketchup part of your fashion statement?"

He groaned, pulled a tissue from his pocket, dampened it and rubbed it against the offending area. Then he looked at her, raised his eyebrows in a question.

"Gone. You are good to go."

"They wanted pancakes and sausage for breakfast," he explained.

"Which would explain the flour fingerprints on your knee." Olivia couldn't stop her laughter when he groaned and bent down to dust off the offending marks.

"Anything else?"

"You do have some green on your shirtfront, but if you put on a jacket it won't show."

Reese muttered something grumpy as he found the mark.

"Pardon?" She couldn't help giggling.

"I said, my jacket's in the car. Hopefully, it's clean." He threw her a disgusted look when she snickered. "You will lose that smile when you see the inside of the house. Promise you won't take it out on me later?"

"No promises."

"I was afraid of that." He shrugged. "Don't try to straighten, okay? It's enough that you're looking after the kids. I have a cleaner coming tomorrow. They'll take care of it."

"Go to work, Reese. Stay as long as you need to. We'll be fine."

He stood silent a moment, then nodded.

"Thank you." He climbed into his car.

"Have a good day."

"It's looking better all the time, Olivia." He met her gaze and held it for a moment. Then he drove away.

Olivia watched his car disappear from sight before she walked inside the house. Her eyes bugged at the mess.

An old adage about idle hands flickered through her mind. No way was she going to have to worry about that today.

Eight-thirty.

Reese rubbed the back of his neck and wondered if he should phone Olivia again.

To say what? That he was going to be even later than he'd promised the last time?

"What are you still doing here, son?" Winifred stood in the doorway looking almost as fresh as she had when he arrived this morning. "Shouldn't you be at home, tucking those little sweethearts of yours into bed?"

Yes, he should be. But instead Reese was stuck here, digging for a solution to a problem he'd created.

"Hi, Grandmother. You're here rather late yourself, aren't you?"

"I had an afternoon nap, doctor's orders." She chuckled. "Whereas you look like you didn't even get a full night's sleep."

"Brett had a nightmare." Reese scrambled for a way to find the answers he needed without telling his secret. "You know the chapel you wanted to include in the Chicago store? Are you still certain about it?"

"More than ever. If there's a chapel on-site, people will want to use it for their weddings. If they do, we get a chance to talk to them about the giant step they're taking and maybe the opportunity to mention God's plan for marriage. The chapel is integral to the new store." Winifred's excitement lit up her eyes. "For so long I've prayed for a chance to share my faith more openly and I believe a chapel is something God will use. Why are you asking?"

"I'm concerned about costs. Renting space on the Magnificent Mile that includes a chapel carries a hefty price tag."

"But that was one of the things you said was so great about the Garver property—the ability to have all the square feet we need." Winifred's flawless temples furrowed. "If I recall correctly, you agreed that was the best part of starting another store—the chance to let God direct things."

He had. But only because that's what she wanted to hear.

"Has something changed, Reese?"

"There have been some snags," he admitted, but stopped when her face went white in that way that meant her heart was acting up again. "We have to be mindful that space there is extremely costly."

"I have no doubt you'll handle that."

She trusted him. It didn't seem to matter that he was only a Woodward by adoption. Winifred, his parents, his siblings—they all felt he was up to the challenge and not one of them had expressed the least doubt about his ability to do his job since he'd come home from law school. The insecurity lay hidden inside him, a by-product of long ago.

Reese let Winifred ramble, hoping it would calm her and give him an idea of something they could cut back on. But according to Winifred, everything she'd dreamed of was in the plans for the Chicago store, especially the chapel.

"You're sure you couldn't just rent a church nearby?"

She gave him the look she often used to quell his sons' rebellions.

"Weddings by Woodwards does not need to rent a church when we can offer our own little chapel. Churches sometimes intimidate people. But they don't mind a chapel. It's a perfect opening to have the kind of talks I want to have with my brides. Why are you asking me these things, Reese? What's the problem?" Her hand trembled as she gripped his desk.

Reese dredged up the cocky grin he always used on her, unwilling to trash the dream she'd treasured for years or add to her anxiety.

"I'm the detail man. That's why you hired me, remember? To cross every T and dot every I. That's what I'm doing, making sure."

"I see." She sat with both feet on the floor, steadily watching him.

Reese heaved a sigh of relief when the phone rang.

"This is a call I've been waiting for. Do you mind if I take it privately?"

"I am the president of Weddings by Woodwards. Surely there aren't any secrets from me?" Winifred said, but she rose and walked to the door as he asked his caller to wait. "When you're ready to talk, Reese, I will listen."

"Thank you, Grandmother." He waited until she'd closed the door behind her. "Go ahead," he said to the bank manager.

"I'm sorry to say this, Reese, but you wanted a second opinion and here it is. I've checked and rechecked the numbers. Weddings by Woodwards is not in a position at the current time to achieve the kind of loan you are considering, as well as pay for the in-store designs already drafted for Chicago. I'm sorry."

"I see." His heart dove to his toes.

"I know how much your grandmother is counting

on this new store. I suggest you begin lease negotiations with the new buyer of the property as soon as possible."

"But there's no guarantee they will lease and if they up the square foot price—" Reese gulped. If none of Winifred's ideas could come true, he'd have failed her. Failed the family. Proven that he wasn't worth the trust they'd placed in him.

Unless he could figure out some way—

"I wish the news was better."

"It's not your fault. I appreciate your help, Tim." Reese paused a moment, lowered his voice. "Please keep this discussion between us. I need time to sort things through."

"Of course. I'll add my prayers, too."

"Great." Reese swallowed his bitter response about his doubt that God would help. He hadn't so far.

The full impact of the call hit home.

He'd messed up.

Him. Nobody else.

Because of his impossible demands. He'd refused to accept the lease they offered, revising points that already met most of Granny Winnie's demands. And why? Because he wanted to prove himself to them.

But if Reese couldn't work this out, Weddings by Woodwards, his grandmother's prized company, which thrived on a reputation of excellence, would have to settle for a location far less deluxe than her dream. Or Winifred would have to let go of her dream completely. The newspapers would eat up the news that Woodwards was scaling back the new store, especially if it coincided with his grandmother's debut of her fall collection. Sales would no doubt take a hit.

But that wasn't the worst part.

The worst part was that Reese's mistake meant everyone in the company would see how stupidly he'd messed up—him, the guy who was always ragging the staff about details. Even if he asked every person on the payroll to forgo their bonuses and the company dipped into its emergency reserve fund, which was already extremely low, even if he and the rest of the family chipped in privately, it was highly unlikely that he could secure the Garver property.

Everyone would suffer because of his mistake.

Reese couldn't let that happen. He was the company lawyer, trusted by the Woodwards family and its employees to protect the company's best interests. He was the guy who prized security, who constantly strove to make sure nothing bad happened and if it did, to have a cushion ready. He was the guy who, ever since Taylor's death, made sure he never needed to count on anyone else for help.

All the years of trying to show he was worthy of the family's trust could be wiped out by this one mistake.

Reese wasn't going to let that happen. For the moment, this was going to be his problem. Reese would take care of it on his own.

And if he failed?

Reese squeezed his eyes shut, thought about the boys and how they reveled in the family's love, how secure they felt among the family, how that security had cushioned the loss of their mother. His primary goal had always been to ensure his children were sheltered enough that they never felt beholden to anyone. Not the way he felt beholden to the family that had rescued him all those years ago. Now he wondered if his mistake would jeopardize the boys' security with his family.

The idea was untenable. But so was imagining the family's disappointment when they learned that his stupidity had cost them the Chicago store. There had to be a way out. He simply needed to figure it out. But not tonight.

Reese shut down his computer, picked up his suit jacket and left the office. As he drove home he tried to pray. But whatever connection he'd had with God had long since dissipated. The family would disagree, but Reese knew God had abandoned him.

For now he'd just have to manage this latest problem as he had all the others.

Alone.

Chapter Four

"**I**'m sorry, Mrs. Woodward, but Reese isn't here at the moment."

"To whom am I speaking?" Fiona Woodward's voice sounded troubled.

"This is Olivia Hastings."

"Olivia! My dear, I've been meaning to call you and thank you for saving Brett. When I think what could have happened, it makes me shudder."

"Me, too. I'm just glad I was there. Can I give Reese a message from you when he comes in?"

"No. I won't trouble him again tonight. I'll wait till morning. Good to talk to you, Olivia. Perhaps we can have lunch one day soon."

"I'd like that."

"So would I, my dear."

Olivia hung up the phone and turned, stifling her small shriek as she caught sight of and recognized the figure in the doorway.

"You scared me," she said, lifting a hand to quiet her thumping heart. "I didn't hear you come in."

"Good thing you didn't." Reese made a face. "I cannot deal with Fiona tonight."

Fiona—not "my mother."

Frustration? Irritation? Olivia struggled to decipher the storm clouds darkening his eyes as he flung his jacket over one of the counter stools and dropped his briefcase beside it.

"Did you eat dinner?"

"No." He pulled out the container of milk and poured himself a huge glass. "I'll have this instead. Kids okay?"

"Sleeping." She took the glass from him and set it on the breakfast bar. "I kept a plate warm for you. Why don't you have the milk with it?"

"You didn't have to do that, but thank you."

Olivia shifted, suddenly shy under his intent stare. She drew in a calming breath when Reese glanced away. He eased onto one of the chrome stools before he dragged a hand through his hair.

"I'm starving. Mac and cheese or hot dogs— which is it?"

"Are those your favorite foods?" Olivia paused in the midst of unwrapping her foil covered dish. "If I'd known I wouldn't have made this. Only the steak was already thawed and I thought—sorry," she mumbled, feeling stupid as she set the plate in front of him.

"Sorry? Are you kidding me? This looks and smells delicious." He cut off one corner of the meat, popped it in his mouth and groaned. "Fantastic! I didn't know you were a gourmet cook, too."

"I'm not. It's just Swiss steak and mashed potatoes. Nothing fancy." She grinned, sat down beside him. "You did seem to have rather a lot of potatoes peeled."

"Ha." As he ate, Reese studied her. "I'm amazed you're still standing after such a long day with the imps. You'll certainly sleep tonight."

"They're wonderful children. You've done a good job."

His expression remained unreadable.

"Thanks." He glanced around. "Where's Emily?"

"Nelson stipulated that she absolutely had to be home by seven, so I sent her in a cab. I checked and she did arrive safely." Because Olivia didn't think he needed another cup of coffee, she filled the kettle and switched it on. "She's great with the boys."

"Yeah, she is. I should pay you for the cab." Reese reached for his wallet, but his hand froze. "I should," he repeated, "but I can't. I forgot to go to the ATM."

"It doesn't matter." Olivia rinsed the teapot with hot water while he lifted another bit of steak to his mouth and chewed.

"It does matter. I'll pay you back, I promise. Did you find out what's up with Emily?"

"No. Once we arrived here, she completely changed. I sent out a few probes but she didn't want to talk about it. I thought it was better to let her have a few hours' peace."

"Probably a good idea."

"She tried not to show it, but she wasn't eager to go home."

"Would you be eager to live with Nelson?" His tone was dry.

"Good point. You sounded down when you came in." Olivia dropped two tea bags in the pot, added water and then carried it to the island. She retrieved two cups before sitting down beside him. When he didn't respond, she tried again. "I don't want to pry, but is anything wrong?"

His head jerked up. He frowned at her, his gorgeous blue eyes narrowing. "Why do you ask?"

"Because I want to help, if I can."

"How could you help?"

No disguising the sharp tone in his voice or the tense set of his shoulders. Something obviously *was* wrong. Olivia kept her voice soft.

"I won't know until you tell me the problem, will I?" She waited a moment. When he didn't answer, she continued. "Maybe I can't do a thing. But it often helps to talk things out. I promise you I'm a good listener."

"I'm sure you are." Reese lifted his half-finished plate, dumped the contents in the garbage and set the plate in the dishwasher. "Thanks. That was delicious."

"Are you interested in dessert?" She lifted the cake dome to show him her lopsided effort. "Pineapple upside down cake. It's not gourmet or anything, but—"

"I'm sure it's delicious. Can I taste it later?"

"Sure." Olivia replaced the lid, picked up the two mugs of tea and followed him into the family room. It was clear that whatever the problem, Reese was not ready to tell her. Maybe it had to do with the business.

"Wow! I haven't seen this floor for ages. You shouldn't have cleaned, Olivia." He accepted a cup, frowning at her before he flopped into the big recliner she'd used to settle the boys. It was the perfect place to recite the story of Moses and the Egyptian princess.

"The twins helped. We made it a game and they learned how to put stuff away. Making the cake was their reward." She sat down opposite him, sipped from her cup then set it down, suddenly nervous. "I hope you don't mind."

"Of course not. They should learn to help. Fiona made all of us pick up after ourselves. I've been trying to teach the boys, but sometimes it's easier to do it myself." He sighed, stared into the black television screen. "I don't want all my time with them to be about chores so I slack off on the discipline. I know I shouldn't, but—" He shrugged.

"I don't believe there are any 'shoulds' when it comes to parenting. Each child is different, has different needs. Every parent has to find their own way and that's not always easy. Seems like there should be a book of rules, doesn't it? If you do this, your child will do this." Olivia shook her head. "Unfortunately, relationships don't go by the book."

She stopped, suddenly aware of the silence and of how much she'd said. Reese was studying her with an odd look.

"It sounds like you've been there. Do you have children, Olivia?"

She swallowed hard, struggled for composure.

"No." *Not anymore.*

"Must be your education talking, then." He grinned. "Maybe more education is what I need to equip me to handle those two live wires."

"You don't need another degree, Reese. You love them. That's all Brett and Brady need. Just make sure they always know it."

"I try."

Silence yawned between them. Olivia could see tiredness in the droop of his shoulders and the lines around his eyes. Reese needed to rest. She needed to leave.

"I'd better go." She carried her cup to the kitchen and set it in the dishwasher. "The boys said they go to preschool tomorrow and needed a lunch so we packed one for each. They're in the fridge. They also chose their clothes, which are lying ready in their room."

"Thank you very much, Olivia. I can't tell you how much I appreciate your help today."

Her breath quickened as she realized Reese had followed her. Olivia didn't understand the hum of electricity that vibrated between them. She only knew she was entirely too aware of the pulse beating in his neck, of the tanned strength in his arms, of the fruity aroma the herbal tea left on his breath. And that she needed to keep him at arm's length.

Olivia didn't look up as she grabbed her bag and her keys.

"You're more than welcome. I enjoyed it." She walked toward the front door quickly, hoping she didn't look like she was running away. "Well, good night," she whispered as she grasped the doorknob.

The words died in her throat when his big, warm palm slid over hers.

"Drive carefully, Olivia," he said as he drew the door open.

When she'd reached her car, she risked one look back. Reese leaned against the doorjamb, hair mussed and glowing gold in the porch light. He lifted a hand and she waved back before climbing into her car.

But as she drove away, her heart gave a wistful tug. The day had been so much fun. She hadn't laughed and giggled like that in ages. Tucking in two damp, wiggling bodies, listening to bedtime prayers, receiving their sloppy good-night kisses—she longed to do it over again every night.

Thoughts of adoption awakened in her mind.

"And exactly where would you bring a child?" she asked herself as she drove. "You live in rented accommodations far too small for busy children."

That was easily solved. Her job at Byways was exactly what she wanted. Denver was a city of potential that held none of the heartrending memories of New York. She could settle here. It really was time to start again.

"Thank You, Father," she whispered as she pulled into her parking space. "Thank You for helping me face the future. Could You help Reese tonight, Lord? He seemed so alone."

Olivia walked into her condo, but she didn't turn on any lights. Instead she went out to the deck and sat there in the silence. The stars were out tonight, thousands of them glittering against the black velvet robes of heaven.

Anika had loved stargazing with her daddy.

"Good night, baby," Olivia whispered. "I love you."

The stars twinkled in a dazzling display, but no high-pitched voice squealed with delight when one silver pinprick arced across the heavens and blazed into a shimmering ball of luminance.

"I love you, Trev. And miss you."

No strong supportive arm rested reassuringly against her shoulders. No one answered back, "I love you, too, Liv."

The ache was still there. But for a few brief moments today, Olivia had forgotten all she had lost and buried herself in the exuberant lives of two boys and a young girl.

It was a beginning.

Reese climbed the stairs to Byways as if drawn by a powerful magnet.

He'd come here every day for the past week, addicted to the echoes of laughter and fun he found inside. Even Nelson's simmering discontent couldn't stem the tide of joy that drowned Reese's cares when he entered the youth center.

Running from problems didn't solve a thing. Reese knew that. But coming to Byways, watching Olivia interact with the kids—it was like a fix that his body craved. Each time he stood here and listened, his problems slid into the background and he left feeling more focused, clearer in his resolve to fix the Chicago problem himself.

It was his responsibility and he would handle it. That's what he did at Weddings by Woodwards. He handled things so the family could be free to do what they did best, which was arrange weddings.

"You're frowning, Reese. We don't allow frowns here." Olivia smiled at him before bending to greet the twins who enthusiastically hugged her, mussing her immaculate hairstyle with their busy hands. "Did you come for the boat-making class?" she asked Brett.

"You're gonna make a boat, in here?" His eyes grew enormous.

Emily appeared in the hallway and the boys raced toward her, questions tumbling from their mouths.

"I thought you'd decided to cut back on the outside excursions?" Reese frowned. Boat-making? At this rate the budget would—

"We're making to-scale sailboats that the kids will

test on water at a place and date yet to be determined. Come and see."

Reese followed Olivia's slim figure into the gym, marveling at how fresh she looked even though the thermometer had broken all records for heat the past few days.

"Listen," she whispered, indicating an older man at the front of the room who was demonstrating how to adjust a piece of paper so it resembled a sail.

The twins hunched over a table, watching Emily patiently mimic the folds. Reese's gaze was drawn back to Olivia, who moved quietly around the room, lending a hand where needed, offering a bit of encouragement without disturbing the speaker.

After a time Olivia stepped out of the room. She glanced over her shoulder, as if to ask if Reese wanted to follow. He did. He couldn't get enough of the changes she'd made in the place. He couldn't get enough of her. Emily signaled she'd watch the twins so he followed Olivia.

Downstairs, a group of teens were boisterously learning the physics behind kite flying. They giggled and laughed, good-naturedly ribbing each other.

"Are they always like that?"

"Yes. They're teenagers. You'd better get used to it, Dad." Olivia grinned, then pointed out the group in the backyard with Nelson, practicing tennis.

"How's he been?" Reese followed her to the kitchen.

Olivia didn't answer immediately. Instead, she pulled two bags of lemons out of the fridge and began cutting them in half. Reese watched for a moment then slid the knife from her pale small fingers.

"Let me do this."

"Thanks." Olivia pulled out a juicer and began extracting the lemon juice, her face serene. "Nelson, you mean? He's fine."

"Nelson—fine?" Reese did a double take and wondered how Olivia managed to keep a straight face. "He's not still giving you grief?"

"Actually, Nelson has a wonderful rapport with all the kids. He seldom has to discipline anyone, which is quite amazing when you consider the number of kids here."

She was supporting the guy? Reese couldn't quite figure out Olivia Hastings. Nelson did nothing but bad-mouth her to any board member who would listen. Yet here she was championing her enemy.

"You don't have to stick up for him." The knife cracked loudly against the cutting board. Reese unclenched his fingers to release the tension that burbled up inside. "I've heard about his diatribes against you. I'm sure it makes your job harder."

"Sometimes I have to come across as the heavy." Olivia shrugged as if it didn't bother her. "I'll survive."

"Why?"

"Why what?" She lifted her head and stared at him, her almond-shaped eyes a confusing whirl of greens and brown with flecks of gold glinting in the afternoon light. Lemon juice now spattered the front of her ivory blouse, but even that didn't spoil the attractive picture she made in the shaft of sunlight that poured through the window.

"You have great credentials. You have lots of experience, way more than you need in this place. You could work anywhere. Why do you stay at Byways when Nelson makes it so miserable for you, Olivia? The other directors all left."

"Because this is where God wants me to be." She smiled at him, then went back to squeezing lemons.

"How do you know that?" Reese felt like a dog gnawing a bone, but he couldn't let go it. He had to learn why she was so content.

"I told you I couldn't take the job immediately because I had to pray about it, remember?"

He nodded.

"The truth is that from the moment I stepped through that door, I was almost certain God wanted me to be at Byways."

"Then why—?" He had no business questioning her. But she had so much faith in God. For a moment Reese almost wished he shared it.

"Why didn't I accept right away? I had to be certain, Reese. I had to know that it wasn't my will I was going on and calling it God's. It's easy to do that, you know. If we want something badly, we can make ourselves believe it's what we should have when the truth is, it may not be what we need at all."

"Okay." He wasn't sure he understood exactly what she was saying.

"Don't cut that lemon." She worked quickly, squeezing every half that he'd cut, then tossing all the halves in the garbage. "I love kids. I love working with them."

That was obvious.

"But liking something doesn't necessarily mean God wants me here." She took the knife from him and sliced the last lemon into rings. "I'm determined to make my will bend to God's, so that means I need to step back and wait for his voice in my heart. Then I'm less likely to make mistakes."

She was a confusing mix and he wanted to know more about her.

"Have you always been around kids?"

Olivia's chuckle rang to the rafters as she filled a large pail with water.

"I was an only child. My parents were overprotective biologists who thought knowledge would give their little girl all she needed in the big, bad world."

He wrinkled his nose. "Sounds boring."

"Maybe a little. They died when I was young."

"How did you get into psychology?"

"I wanted to follow my parents, but psychology was the only *science* I enjoyed. I switched from botanical studies to psychology two days into my first semester in college." She mixed lemon juice and sugar into the water and stirred vigorously. "Want to taste?"

"I won't be much help. I've never tasted real lemonade."

Olivia stared at him for a moment as if she couldn't believe he'd been so deprived. Then she smiled. It was like watching the sun reappear.

"You're in for a treat. How about if you get a bag of ice from the freezer and add it? That will chill it till break time. The ice is downstairs in the freezer."

Reese nodded and went to fetch it. As he climbed back up the steps he heard Nelson's angry voice.

"But we're supposed to have ice cream sundaes. I told you that yesterday."

"Yes, you did. But since we already have an ice cream event this week, I thought variety would be better. I baked some cookies to go with the lemonade." No hint of anger colored Olivia's calm response.

"Isn't that nice?" Nelson growled.

"I think it was very considerate of Olivia to take time to bake cookies." Reese strolled into the room. "I haven't had a homemade cookie in ages." He opened the bag and carefully added ice to the pail, taking care not to splash Olivia.

"Is that enough?"

"Yes. Thank you." She added the lemon slices and a few red cherries.

"You're welcome."

Nelson glanced from Olivia to Reese and rolled his eyes.

"Aren't you two just the sweetest? I feel sick," he said, pretending to gag.

"Perhaps it's from lack of manners," Reese said softly, meeting his glare.

Nelson backed off, but not far.

"I suppose she's been telling you all kinds of stuff about me, trying to get me fired."

The venom in the glare Nelson shot his boss would have melted lesser women. Olivia seemed undisturbed by it as she laid out glasses, trays of cookies and a heap of napkins.

"Actually, Olivia was just telling me you had a great rapport with the kids who come here." Reese waited for that to sink in.

Nelson frowned, glancing from her to him darkly.

"What does that mean?" he demanded, suspicion frosting his voice.

"I assumed she meant you get along with the kids. Why would you think it meant anything else?" Reese waited for his response. When it didn't come, he shrugged and pointed upward. "I'm going to check on the twins. Then I'll help serve this stuff."

"You don't have to." But Olivia's smile told him she would be happy to have his help.

"Back in a jiffy." He left, sidestepping Nelson, who looked confused and angry and the tiniest bit uncertain. It was not a look Reese had seen him wear before. Maybe the guy needed a little unsettling to get rid of that colossal chip on his shoulder.

Though the lecturer had finished his talk, most of the students still worked at their paper sails. The twins were arguing with Emily.

"But I don't want to have white sails," Brett complained.

"I do," Emily said firmly. "And it's my boat. When you make your own you can color them black if you want."

"No!" Brett glared at her, his face turning a blotchy rage-red. "I don't like you. You're mean."

Reese saw the small hand reach out toward Emily's paper and reacted quickly, grabbing the chubby fingers before they could do any damage.

"What are you doing, Brett?" he asked in his sternest voice.

Emily backed away, her face paler than Reese had ever seen it.

"I'm s-sorry," she whispered.

"You have nothing to be sorry about. But someone else does." He stared hard at Brett. "You owe Emily an apology."

"No!" Brett glared at him, defiance oozing.

Reese felt the stares of many eyes penetrating his back. He preferred to discipline his children in private whenever possible, but this time a little public shame might press home the point to Brett better than any words he could say.

"Yes, son, you do. You will apologize to Emily. She is your friend. She allowed you to work on her sail because she's kind and generous. We do not repay her kindness with rudeness. We don't speak to our friends or to anyone else the way you did. And we never, ever try to ruin something that belongs to someone else. Do we?"

Brett glared at him, but soon noticed the disapproving stares of the children who'd gathered around to watch. Reese lowered his voice.

"Friendships are precious, son. We take care of them. We are on our best behavior with our friends."

"Why?" Brett tilted his head to one side curiously.

"Because friends, good friends like Emily, are hard to find. And we don't ever want to lose them." He hunkered down to look Brett in the eye. "We all need friends. Friends are a special treasure and we have to be very careful that we never, ever hurt a friend. Emily is your friend. You don't want her to be hurt, do you, Brett?"

"N-no." He wasn't quite convinced.

"Most of the time Emily does what you want. She doesn't say, 'Oh, Brett, I don't feel like jumping on the trampoline right now.' Does she?"

Brady shook his head from side to side.

"Em'ly always jumps with us on the tramp. And when we play blocks she always builds a house exactly the way Brett says." Brady touched Emily's hand tentatively, beamed when her fingers curled around his.

"I know she does. That's because Emily loves you. She doesn't want to do anything to hurt you. She only wants good things for you. Don't you want good things for her? Don't you want her to make her sail the way she wants, Brett?"

Brett looked at the paper he'd been ready to crush. He climbed down from the stool he'd stood on and moved in front of Emily where he paused, staring up at her as if wrestling with a huge problem. After contemplation, he sighed.

"I'm sorry I wasn't nice, Emily."

"It's okay."

"I like having you for my friend. I know you like white way better 'n black 'cause you tole me black makes you sad." He smiled, touched her free hand. "I'm gonna pray you get a white dress just like that one you showed me in your picture."

Emily's cheeks burned red. "Thanks," she muttered, chin sinking into her thin chest.

"S'okay. I want my friend to be happy. Are you happy, Emily?"

"Yes. Thank you, Brett."

"Welcome." He smiled at her and harmony was instantly restored.

Reese told everyone about the lemonade and cookies downstairs, but he insisted the twins wait for him to go with them. Then he turned to Emily.

"Thank you for forgiving them," he said quietly, mindful of her flushed cheeks. "We don't want to lose your friendship."

"Why?" Poor Emily stared at him as if he'd grown two heads. "You can always find another babysitter."

"You're not just a babysitter, Emily. You're special to us, a very good friend who helps me and the twins. We love having you in our lives. I wouldn't ever want you to feel that we hurt you."

"I'm not special." Emily's big eyes studied him as if he were a bug under a microscope. "But I like being with the twins. They make me laugh, and I don't feel stupid."

Stupid? Where had that come from?

Reese was about to ask her when he heard a sound behind him. He turned.

"What's going on here?" Nelson demanded, scowling. "Emily, you're on kitchen duty this week, aren't you?"

"Yes. I'm going now." She scurried away, pausing a second at the top of the stairs to risk a worried glance at her brother.

"Relax, will you, Nelson? She was only talking to me." Reese nodded at the twins that they could go downstairs. "She's very good with young children," he offered, but the other man wasn't buying into his jovial tone.

"Perhaps it seems nothing to you, Reese, but I am responsible for my sister, as well as what happens with activities here at Byways. It's hard to keep things organized and running a certain way here and at home, but I'm trying to teach Emily to live up to her word. She promised to help in the kitchen. Baby-sitting your sons will have to wait."

The self-righteous tone goaded Reese into a response.

"We all want the best for Emily, Nelson. A few minutes talking to the kids won't ruin her, surely?"

It was a great comeback, except in the next instant a resounding crash echoed up from the basement.

"That'll be my two." Reese headed for the stairs,

almost certain he heard Nelson mutter something about poor parenting.

"It sounded worse than it is," Olivia reassured Reese when he stepped through the doorway. "Some of the tins I've been collecting got bumped and that sent the whole works tumbling. Everyone's fine. Aren't we?" she called.

Mouths stuffed with cookies and lemonade hummed agreement.

"It's a wonder parents are ever able to eat," Reese grumbled as he plucked chocolate chips from Brett's hair. "Cleaning up you two is gross."

Brett stuffed the last bite in his mouth, then hurried away to help Emily collect used paper cups.

"Me, too." Brady wiggled out from under Reese's hand and joined them.

"It's a bit like feeding locusts." Olivia giggled as she wiped off the tables. "At least they didn't complain about my cooking."

"These are great." Reese chewed a cookie, savoring the textures of oatmeal and coconut as he watched her.

"I saved you a glass of lemonade." She waited until he tasted it. "Too sour?"

"No. It's just—different than the store-bought kind. I like it," he assured her.

"It's good for you and it has no caffeine and not as much sugar as a lot of sodas." She kept working until the room had been restored to its usual order. "Go ahead outside with the others, Emily. Get some fresh air."

"But Nelson said I'm supposed to help." She looked worried.

"You have. Now go have fun with the others."

Reese wondered what Emily's version of "fun" was, especially with a brother like Nelson. He gave the twins permission to play on the slide. They raced away while he and Olivia walked upstairs at a more sedate pace.

"There's a bench over here. We can watch them from it." She led him there, sat down and patted the warm wood. "Relax for a while. You look like you need it."

"Work's a bit tough right now." He watched the twins for a moment, but his gaze wandered to where Nelson supervised a soccer game. Emily was as far away from her brother as she could get in the outside area. Reese found that curious. "Have you noticed any change in Emily lately?" he asked quietly.

"Change?" Olivia tilted her head to study him. "How?"

"Brett was rude to her. I was disciplining him, and she looked at me like I was going to attack her. It was not a pleasant feeling." He waited, but Olivia remained silent. Reese frowned and tried to read her expression. "What?"

"There is something off with her," she murmured. "I have a hunch I know what's wrong but I don't want to say anything just yet, okay?"

"Why?"

"Because I need to be sure."

"Do you think it's all right to still have her babysit?" he asked, wondering if he'd made a mistake in allowing the twins to spend so much time with Emily. But they adored her. And she'd always seemed perfectly happy with them.

"Of course. Babysitting for you is the highlight of her week. She always talks about it." Olivia's smile reached up into her eyes. "She's very proud that you trust her with them, you know."

"I didn't know." He sat beside her, content to listen to the screams of excitement, the laughter and the occasional burst of tears, which was quickly hushed by one of the other workers. "You're doing good here, Olivia. It's not easy to make a difference in a kid's life, but you're doing it."

"I have a lot of help. But thank you."

"Are the kids opening up more now that you've been here for a while?"

"Mmm-hmm. This morning one of the older ones confided she's afraid to tell her parents she is pregnant."

"That's tough." Reese watched Brady flop onto his stomach to watch an ant. "Don't you ever get defeated?"

"Are you wondering if I'm going to quit?" she teased.

"No. You like it here too much," he said honestly. "It's got to be draining, though."

"Sometimes." She gave him an arch look. "So is parenting. But infinitely rewarding, don't you think?"

Again Reese had the sense that Olivia was speaking from experience.

"Some days are better than others." Reese turned the conversation back on her. "I've heard you talking to the kids here several times. You always project a deep confidence in them. Where does that come from?"

He waited, determined to understand that deep assurance that was so much a part of Olivia Hastings.

"Kids are so vulnerable. They ask so little and they get hurt so badly when someone fails them." Olivia's face glowed with something that had not been applied with this morning's makeup. It came from deep inside. "Do you remember feeling like that, Reese?"

"Yes." She couldn't know that bits of hurt still lurked inside his orphaned heart. But this wasn't about him.

"Most kids need boundaries." Olivia grabbed the ball that landed at her feet and tossed it back. "They also need to be sure that a mistake can be forgiven. Just like with God."

"Okay, you'll have to explain that."

"God grants us a clean slate when we ask Him for forgiveness. We don't have to earn it, or do something to be worthy of it. It's ours. That's what I want the kids here to understand. There are boundaries, but there is also someone who loves them, all the time."

"That's oversimplified, surely?"

"Not at all. That's the whole thing about being in God's family, Reese. It is simple. Until we make it complicated."

"Huh?" Reese felt the surprise in her glance. Like everyone else, Olivia probably figured he should know the answer, but he didn't. And he wanted to.

"We start doubting. Maybe God didn't mean what He said. Maybe I'm all alone here. Maybe I'm not worthy of God's love."

"Aren't doubts normal? The twins often seek re-assurance."

"Exactly." She grinned. "That's what we should do. Ask God and then accept His love. Because there is no way you can prove love. It simply is." Olivia waved a hand at Brett, who was showing off on the swings. "I want the kids that come here to know they are loved even if there is no other human being in their life who tells them that. Maybe if I can show them love, it will help them understand God's love."

Reese thought Olivia's statement astounding. But he didn't get to say that because the twins came roaring up.

"I'm hungry, Daddy."

"Me, too." Brady rubbed his cheek. "And I want a drink."

"You just had cookies and lemonade," Reese protested. He checked his watch.

"An hour ago," Olivia added with a chuckle. "That's what I love most about this job—time flies."

She rose as Nelson ended the game. "I guess I'd better help him."

"Can Olivia have dinner with us, Daddy?" Brady tugged at his hand, eyes glowing. "We like Olivia."

"Thank you, Brady. I like you, too. And Brett." She ruffled his already-tousled hair.

"That's a good idea, son. We do owe her dinner, at the very least." Reese winked at Brady then turned to Olivia. "We'd love to have you join us for dinner, if you don't have other plans. I promise you won't even have to work for your supper."

Something flickered in her eyes as she studied him. He felt a bump of relief when she finally nodded.

"If you're sure it won't put you to too much trouble."

"It won't. The guys will help me. What time's good for you?"

"Name the hour, and I'll be there."

They settled on the time, but before Olivia could leave, Reese held out some money.

"By the way, this is for you. To repay you for Emily's cab fare. I also need to find her." He held up a small envelope. "It's her babysitting money."

"Thanks." Olivia pocketed her cash. "Emily's over there with Nelson. See you later."

Reese watched Olivia hurry up the steps and inside Byways. Then his gaze slid to Emily, who was listening with bent head and slouched shoulders to whatever her brother was saying.

Olivia was right. There was something odd about that relationship. The girl's head suddenly jerked up and she backed away from Nelson. Reese didn't like the way she cowered. Surely Nelson would never strike her.

"Hey, guys. I think we should invite Emily for dinner, too."

"Yippee!"

The twins raced ahead of him, singsonging her name so loudly Nelson stopped speaking and glared at them in annoyance. How the man worked with children was beyond Reese. He seemed to have no patience whatsoever, but maybe that was only with *his* children.

Reese quickly caught up and reissued the twins' invitation.

"You didn't have anything special planned for this evening, did you, Nelson? If I remember, this is your bowling night." If Reese had hoped to earn brownie points with Nelson for remembering the little he'd shared about his life away from Byways, it was not happening.

Nelson remained impassive, inclined his head and frowned. Emily's shoulders drooped, as if she expected a refusal. Or worse.

Reese cleared his throat.

"Your sister did us a big favor helping out Olivia the other day, Nelson. The least I can do is repay her with dinner. Oh, and this is the money I owe you." He held out the envelope.

"Thanks." Emily slid it into a pocket after a quick glance at her brother.

"You're going to cook, Reese?" Nelson made it sound impossible.

"I quite often do. Otherwise we wouldn't eat." He lifted an eyebrow. "Well? Can Emily come?"

"If she wants." Nelson tossed a dismissive glance in his sister's direction. "But I won't be able to pick her up afterward. I'm meeting some friends."

As far as Reese could discern, Nelson and Emily spent very little time together. Given the look on her face, maybe that was a good thing.

"I'll run Emily home. Or Olivia will. Or we'll call a cab again. Don't worry. We'll work something out. That's if you want to come, Emily." He made it a point to wait for her agreement. One heavy in the group was enough. Reese sure didn't want to be compared to Nelson.

"Yes. Please," she whispered after peeking at her brother. "Is it okay?"

"Fine. Go. In fact, you might as well go with him now. I don't know how late I'll be here, closing things down."

Reese itched to point out that there wasn't much left for Nelson to do. While they'd been talking, Olivia had been busy with the other workers putting things away. Most of the kids had pitched in and were now leaving. But he remained silent. Better to keep the peace.

"All right, then." He grinned at Emily. "Let's go. Ready, Em?"

She nodded and let the twins tug her toward the parking lot.

"Have a good evening, Nelson," he called over one shoulder.

"You, too." A snide tone underlaid the remark.

Reese chose to ignore that and unlocked the car. Once the kids were belted into their seats with Emily between, he headed toward the grocery store.

"I sure hope you're as good a shopper as you are a babysitter, Em, because we really need to stock up. I've been putting it off too long."

"I do all our grocery shopping," she told him, her voice quiet. "I'm getting quite good. But I didn't bring my coupon folder. It's always cheaper if you use the coupons from the newspaper, you know. Should we go to my place and pick it up?"

Reese glanced in his rearview mirror, saw she was serious.

"I don't think we have time today, Emily. You point out what you think are the best deals and I'll go with that. Okay?"

"'Cept for the ice cream. We have to get all the stuff for the monster mash ice cream pie 'cause it's our favorite. Right, Daddy?" Brady chirped.

"Yep. Monster mash is the greatest," he agreed, privately reminding himself to pick up some sherbet for Olivia. He was pretty sure his monster mash wouldn't be her first choice for dessert.

Maybe tonight he'd learn more about her.

Chapter Five

Olivia glanced around the table, savoring the giggles and chatter of happy children. How long had it been since she'd shared such a joyous meal?

"More roasted potatoes?" Reese asked her, his face deadpan as he offered the last two golden-brown potatoes sitting on the singed and blackened pan.

"Thank you, no. I couldn't eat another thing. It was all so delicious."

It was the truth. Olivia couldn't recall when last she'd enjoyed a meal more. It wasn't the food, though. She could have been eating sawdust for all the notice she took. It was the laughter, the sharing and the togetherness.

"Then I'll just clear these plates and we'll have dessert. Everyone does want pie, don't they?"

"I do, Daddy," said Brett.

"Me, too," Brady echoed. "An' Em'ly wants some, too."

Emily rushed to help Reese, so Olivia sank back

into her chair, realizing the young girl needed to feel needed. Olivia studied Brett's and Brady's rapt expressions.

"Your dad made pie?" she whispered.

"He's making it now." Brett's answer was hardly a whisper, but then he was excited. "Monster mash pie. It's our favorite."

"Yeah. Favorite." Brady clapped his hands with glee. "Do you like monster mash pie, Olivia?"

"I don't know. I've never tasted it before."

Pie making? Reese Woodward certainly had hidden assets. And the ones that weren't hidden were not bad, either.

"Me first," Brett yelled as his father came into the dining room bearing a tray with three dishes.

"Ladies first," Reese corrected. "This is for Emily." He glanced up, winked at Olivia. "Do you think you'd like to try some of our monster mash pie?"

She stared at the dish he'd set on the table, swallowed hard and met his smirk head-on.

"Actually, I think I'm too full to eat an entire dish. Would it be all right if I sampled Brett's and Brady's—maybe one tiny spoonful from each?" She prayed he understood what she wasn't saying.

Reese grinned and mouthed the word, "chicken" before turning to the boys.

"Guys? Are you going to share with Olivia?"

Brady didn't mind, but Brett wasn't as easily persuaded until Emily stepped in and offered her own dish.

"No, Emily," he said firmly. "You always pick out the carrots. Real monster mash pies have carrots in them. I'll share with Olivia. But just a little share."

"Thank you, Brett. That's very kind." Olivia lifted her spoon and dipped it into the ice cream concoction Brett held out. "Hmm," she said, rolling the creamy lumps on her tongue. "This is really different. Now what do I taste?"

"Peanut butter," Brady squealed.

"It could be the grapes," Emily offered.

"It's definitely not carrot." Olivia struggled to discern flavors.

"Coconut?" Reese suggested, the corner of his mouth tipping up as he watched her sip her water. "No? Raisins? Maybe blueberries? Oh, I know. It's got to be the yogurt we put on the graham crackers."

"Yogurt, yes. That must be it. My, that certainly is a monster mash pie." Olivia licked her lips. Reese's face told her he wasn't buying her act. "I'm sorry that I'm too full to enjoy any more, but you all go ahead. Reese," she said sweetly, "aren't you having any monster mash pie?"

"Daddy's 'llergick so he can't eat it. He got some other stuff. It's not as good as monster mash pie, though." Brett shook his head sadly before diving back into his dessert treat.

"Allergic?" Olivia managed to keep her face deadpan. "That is sad. Which part, exactly, are you allergic to, Reese?"

"That's not important," he said, waving a hand as if swatting at a fly. "I bought some sherbet. Would you like some of that?"

Brett's head jerked up, his face suspicious. Olivia smiled.

"I can't right now, thanks," she said. "Too full, remember? Maybe later."

"Coffee, then," Reese said and left to prepare it.

Drinking their coffee was sidelined until the table was cleared. Emily and the boys volunteered to put the dishes in the dishwasher so Reese led the way out to the deck, carrying a thermal carafe. He set it down on the cedar table and took the cups from her.

"Have a seat," he offered.

"Thanks. Very clever idea with the 'monster mash' ice cream," she complimented. "Potato peeling and now monster mash ice cream. You should be the one working at Byways with the success you've had here."

He actually blushed.

"I had to do something. They wouldn't eat certain foods because some kid at preschool told them a silly story. I simply came up with a better one."

"Must have been a doozie," she chuckled.

"I may only be a boring lawyer, but I do have my strengths." Reese preened a moment before pouring. With one cup full, he paused, lifted his head and closed his eyes, head tilted to one side. "Notice anything?"

Olivia frowned, closed her eyes, too, trying to figure out his meaning. "No."

"Silence," he murmured.

She blinked and caught him grinning at her.

"Well, relative silence," he amended with a jerk of his thumb toward the open kitchen window overlooking the far end of the patio. Childish chatter was faintly discernable. "I haven't heard a major crash or anyone crying, so that's good."

"It's lovely out here." She sipped her coffee and studied the flowering hedges surrounding the yard. "Are you the gardener?"

"Grandmother. I am merely her obedient slave. She insisted I do something to turn our muddy hole into a backyard for the kids." His dour expression made her laugh. "Last year she made me slave out here for two of the hottest weeks of the summer to finish every detail. But she was right. The hedges hide the fence while giving us security and privacy. The kids can play out here and I know they'll be safe."

"How long have you lived here?" Olivia hoped Reese wouldn't think she was prying, but she wanted to know more about him and his sons.

"A couple of years. I bought this place a few months after Taylor died. We were in a great town house, but I didn't like being so far from work. Especially when I had to leave the boys with a sitter." He had been studying the contents of his cup, but now he lifted his head, met her gaze. "My wife was killed by a drunk driver."

"I'm sorry. It's hard to understand why those we love have to die, isn't it?" That was as close as Olivia wanted to get to discussing her own past.

"You've lost someone?" Reese's face hid in the shadows. The solar lights around the yard had come on, but they weren't bright enough to allow her to read his expression.

"Yes." Olivia scrambled for a change of subject and came up blank.

"I'm sorry."

"So am I. It's taken a while, but I'm getting better. My faith has helped."

"It has?" His posture shifted. He leaned forward. "How?"

"Well, for one thing, I finally accepted that God is in control and whatever He does is for my good."

Reese barked out a laugh that held no amusement.

"What's so funny?"

"How can losing someone I loved, the mother of two small innocent boys, no less, do anyone any good?"

Her heart pinched tight at the pain and anger in his voice. Olivia knew exactly how he felt, how deep the questions went, how hard the answers were to accept.

"I didn't say I could explain it," she murmured. "I said I accepted that God is in control. That means my hands are off the situation. It's up to Him. That is very hard, but it's what He requires of us if we truly trust Him. And I do."

"Trust—no matter what?"

Olivia nodded.

"I don't understand how you can trust someone who takes everything and leaves you to face life on your own." Reese kept his face averted, hiding his pain inside.

"But that's not what God does," Olivia protested. "God didn't leave you alone, Reese. He left you with two boys who adore you, a family who loves and cares for you, who want to help. He left you with His spirit to comfort you and the knowledge that your wife is with the person who loves her even more than you did."

"God took what I loved and abandoned me. Now He expects me to manage on my own." Reese shook his head. "Tell me, Olivia, why do I need God?"

"God never abandoned you."

"It sure feels like it," Reese muttered.

"Neither does He expect you to manage on your own. Far from it. God expects you to trust Him enough to realize that He makes all things work together for good." His pain was tangible in the night air, and Olivia couldn't help but reach out to touch him, to offer some measure of comfort. She slipped her hand over his.

"For good?" he scoffed. "A broken family—how can that be good?"

"What kind of God do you believe in, Reese? A God who punishes people, who steals away what they love? Or do you believe in the God of the Bible, who wants to be loved and adored because He loves and adores us? You have to figure that out first."

"Why?" His hand slid from under hers and hid it under the table. "What does it matter what I believe about God?"

"It matters a great deal." Olivia whispered a prayer for help. "If your view of God isn't right, how can you have a right relationship with Him? The Bible says in Philippians, 'Work out your salvation with fear and trembling.'"

"So God will be whatever I want Him to be?" Reese's husky voice brimmed with anger. "That's convenient."

"God is who He is, Reese, *not* who you want Him to be. But you have to accept that God can't go against Himself, that He can't lie. He said He loves us." How could she explain what she'd only begun to understand? "Do you believe that?"

"I don't know anymore."

"Well, that's what Philippians is saying. Figure out who you believe God is. You can't accept someone else's viewpoint or relationship. You have to forge your own beliefs from what the Bible teaches and the promises He's given." Olivia ached for the confusion filling his face.

"I thought we're supposed to accept what we were taught in church."

"Most churches do teach the basic tenets of Christian faith. But there's more to being a believer. You need to have a personal relationship with God, the same as you have with humans. You have to get to know God, who He is, what He thinks." Olivia leaned forward, determined to help him as someone else had helped her. "Once you understand who God is and what He wants for us, you must hang on to that knowledge."

"It's hard to do when He lets the worst happen."

"Maybe, but you can't doubt Him every time hard times come around, Reese. No more than you can doubt your grandmother's love when she asks you to do something hard or costly. Faith means believing God is who He says He is even when we don't see it."

"So how do you reconcile God allowing your loved ones to die, Olivia?" Reese's voice, harsh and brimming with anger, fractured the evening's serenity. "Explain that."

Olivia shook her head.

"I can't. I'm not God. I can't possibly understand His mind or plans." She struggled to clarify her words before she spoke again. "I can't explain what happened to you or to me, Reese, or why. But I'm certain that God loves me, and because He is a God of love, there was a reason for them to die."

"And that's enough for you?"

"For now."

"It isn't enough for me, Olivia."

Her heart ached at the words, but the chance to say more was gone with the arrival of the twins and Emily, who begged Reese to light a fire in the pit.

"A small one," Reese relented after an unsuccessful attempt to talk the boys out of the idea. "For a short time. Then you're going to bed without arguing. Correct?"

"Yes, Daddy," they repeated, their little faces beaming with anticipation.

Whatever heartache lay buried inside, Reese seemed determined his sons and Emily not detect it. He directed the boys to gather wood chips from the pile of wood hidden under the deck. Emily scoured for dry bits of bark. Reese even gave Olivia a part in getting the fire started.

"Your job is to squish up this newspaper." His grin begged her to forget their discussion. "The tighter it is, the longer it takes to burn. But don't rub it on your clothes or you'll get really dirty."

"As if that matters." She began squishing, enjoying Emily's latest knock-knock jokes.

With the paper, bark and chips assembled, father and sons gathered around the pit as Reese explained how to get the fire going. Emily sat beside Olivia, her eyes on the twins who were allowed to toss in one piece of kindling each once the tinder had caught.

"I like it when you laugh, Olivia. You're pretty."

"Thank you, Emily. I like it when you laugh, too. Your eyes sparkle."

"Sometimes there's not much to laugh at," the girl admitted very quietly. "That's why I always remember the knock-knock jokes. So I can make myself smile."

Such a sad thing to admit. Olivia knew she'd have to tread carefully if she wanted to learn what was behind Emily's forlorn words.

"Do you like coming to Byways, Emily?"

"I love it!" The thin face blazed with joy. But as quickly the flash fire in her eyes had been doused. "Most of the time, anyway."

"What don't you like?" Olivia asked, pretending great interest in her almost empty cup. "I've been asking everyone to give me ideas about what to change at Byways."

"Oh. Well." Emily frowned. "I wish it was open on Saturdays."

"It will be during the school year. But in the summer we have such full days—" Olivia stopped. *Don't justify. Learn.* "What would you like to do on Saturdays, Emily?"

"Learn new things. Like me and my friend Sylvia, you know her?" Emily described a girl she frequently chummed with.

"Yes, I know who she is."

"Well, Sylvia's like me. She's alone a lot. Her mom and dad work, so she has to make dinner lots of nights. Like me. I wish we could take some cooking lessons. There's a grocery store that offers them on Saturdays, but—" Emily stopped, bit her lip as she obviously rethought what she'd been about to say. "It's too far for me and Sylvia to go alone."

"Maybe if you asked Nelson, he'd drop you off. I'm sure he'd appreciate better cooking, wouldn't he?"

"No!" Emily looked terrified. "I thought you were talking about doing stuff at Byways."

"You're right, we were." Olivia mentally kicked herself for mentioning Nelson. "Okay, what other kinds of things would you like to do on Saturdays?"

"Learn how to sew a dress and play the guitar. Have somebody show me how to make my hair pretty. Stuff like that." Emily's head rested on her chest. But after a moment she peeked upward through her long bangs. "Silly, isn't it?"

"No, I think it's a great list of things. I can get tons of ideas from that. Thanks."

"Hey, are you girls afraid of a bit of wood smoke?" Reese called.

"Emily's not afraid of anything," Brett chirped. "Are you, Emily?"

The young girl's cheeks pinkened. She risked a look at Olivia as they left the deck and moved nearer the fire.

"I guess I am afraid of some things, Brett," she murmured. "Everybody's afraid of something."

"Not Daddy. He's not afraid of nothing. Are you, Daddy?"

"Well, son." Reese waited until Emily and Olivia were seated in the chairs around the fire before sinking down into his own. He studied his little boy in the flickering light, his tone very soft. "I guess there are some things I'm afraid of, too."

"You're a scaredy-cat?" Brady seemed shocked.

"What are you scared of, Daddy?" Brett frowned at him.

"I get scared when you and Brady don't obey me."

"Why does that get you scared?" Brett frowned.

"Because I don't want you to be hurt. That's why I make rules, because I want to protect you guys." He reached out and ruffled Brett's hair, chucked him under the chin. "Mostly though, I'm afraid you'll grow up too fast and I won't get to do all the things with you that I want."

"I'm four," Brady told him solemnly. "I'm not growing up too fast."

"Almost five," Brett corrected. He thought for a moment. "If we do one thing every day we'll have enough time before you get too old, Daddy."

Olivia had to smother her grin behind her hand.

"Thank you, son. That's reassuring."

They chatted back and forth as the fire waned, but soon yawns interspersed the conversation.

"Bedtime." Reese rose.

"Aw, Dad."

"You promised, Brett," Emily reminded.

"I know." Brett sighed, but after a glance at his father's face he trudged toward the house. At the deck he turned back. "Do I have to have a bath?"

"Too tired, huh?" Reese inclined his head. "How about a shower? It's quick and the dirt still gets washed away."

Brett thought about it for a minute. "I'll get water in my eyes."

"Not if you close them, silly." Emily looked at Reese. "I'll help them. Then you and Olivia can visit some more."

"Hey, Em, I didn't ask you for dinner so you could babysit. And I'm sure you don't want to get soaked to the skin by these two munchkins." Reese knocked down the fire so it was mostly coals. "I'll do it."

"Please? I don't mind." She looked so earnest, her hand reaching for Brett's as they waited for Reese's permission. "I promise I'll watch them very carefully."

"If you have any trouble you call me from the bathroom. Don't leave the boys, okay?" When she agreed, Reese nodded and the three raced into the house, slamming the screen door behind them. "I feel like a slave driver," he admitted as he sank down in the chair next to Olivia.

"Why? You heard her. Emily loves being with them." Olivia paused, frowned. "Unless…don't you trust her?"

"Of course I trust her. Otherwise I'd never let her babysit them." His head jerked around and he stared at her. "Where did that come from?"

"I just realized—it must be hard to let the twins out of your sight, after what you've gone through, I mean." Embarrassed by her probing, Olivia fixed her gaze on the last glowing embers of the fire. "I think I'd be terrified."

"I was afraid of losing them at first." He leaned forward, elbows propped on his knees. "I even took them to work with me until Grandmother insisted neither of us were happy with the situation. They need to run and play and be with other kids. I needed to work. The preschool and the day care suit us fine for now."

"And soon they'll start school."

"Yes." He didn't sound excited.

Since Reese seemed disinclined to talk about his private affairs any more, Olivia chose several other topics for conversation. His desultory responses did little to encourage further conversation. She'd almost decided it was time to leave when Reese suddenly turned to her.

"I'm sorry. I'm being a lousy host. Chalk it up to a crappy day."

"You've said that before." Olivia felt as if she were tiptoeing around those bushes he'd planted. "Is something wrong at Woodwards? It might help to talk about it. I can keep a secret, if that's what you need."

"Why would you think I have a secret?" Dark eyes searched hers in the firelight.

"Something's troubling you. I'm just offering to be a listener if you need one."

The patio door slid open.

"The boys are asking you to kiss them good-night," Emily said. "Both of you," she added when Reese rose.

"I'm flattered." Olivia followed them inside, whispering a plea for help to get through the next few minutes.

Sure enough, old memories surged up like fiery volcanoes when four chubby arms circled her neck and sloppy kisses landed halfway between her cheek and her chin, but thankfully, Reese kept things to a minimum. The boys' eyes were closed before they left the room.

"It was a lovely evening, Reese, thank you."

"You're welcome. I'm glad you came. And you, Emily. It was nice of you to bathe the boys. They love having you here."

"I like coming here." Emily's face was almost hidden in her neck. "It's a happy place."

Olivia shared a look with Reese before she retrieved her purse.

"I think it's time I took you home," she said.

Emily frowned, but didn't disagree so they left quickly, eager not to disturb the boys. While Emily climbed into the car, Olivia grabbed the last opportunity to speak to Reese.

"If you need to talk, you have my number," she said softly. "I won't judge, Reese. I won't offer advice. I'll just listen. Sometimes it helps to share."

"Thanks." He held her door, waited till she was seated inside, then bent. "Come again," he invited, his eyes holding hers. Then he shifted to smile at Emily. "You, too."

"I will." Emily snapped her seat belt into place as Reese closed Olivia's car door.

Olivia waved once before she backed out and drove away. Emily remained quiet on the ride home, offering only monosyllabic responses. Her home loomed dark and scary in the night shadows. That ir-

ritated Olivia. At least Nelson could have left on a
light. Emily was only thirteen.

"Shall I come in with you?" She didn't wait for a
response. Emily's expression of relief was enough.
Inside, once they'd switched on some lights and determined all was safe, Olivia took note. The house
was picture-perfect, too perfect. There wasn't a
speck of dust on any surface. No books strewn
around or jackets tossed on a chair.

Maybe Nelson had a housekeeper?

"I can stay if you need me to," she offered, noting
Emily's hurried glance out the window.

"No, thanks. I'm fine. I'm used to being alone."
Emily's voice wobbled, but she smiled gallantly,
refusing to admit her worries. "Nelson will be back
soon."

"Leave on the outside light." Olivia wished Emily
didn't have to stay alone so much. "Thanks for
coming today."

"I had fun."

"I'm glad," she whispered as she hugged the
girl. "You deserve some fun. Good night, sweetie.
Sleep well."

"You, too."

Olivia drove home with the picture of Emily's
pinched face lingering in her mind. Too disturbed to
relax, she made herself a cup of tea and went outside
to sit in the moonlight. At the moment, prayers were
all she could do for the lonely girl. Convinced more
than ever that there was something wrong in Emily's

world, Olivia prayed, asking for help for the young girl and her brother.

Some time later the phone rang.

"Am I disturbing you?" Reese asked.

"Not at all. I'm sitting in the dark, watching the stars."

"Me, too." Silence yawned between them. "You really don't mind if I unload on you?"

"Of course not. Nobody can keep everything bottled up, and you're carrying a pretty heavy load, Reese."

"Thanks." A sigh. "I have some problems at work," he admitted, his voice tight with strain. "I don't want the family to know about them. Yet."

"They wouldn't understand?" Olivia wasn't sure where to go with this. The Woodwards seemed a most loving family.

"It's not that."

She was glad he'd called. There had been a connection between them from the moment they'd met. At first she'd been afraid to explore it, but now that Reese seemed to need her she couldn't deny that she enjoyed the chance to speak with him. If she could help, she was more than willing.

Besides, no one had bothered her here. Maybe it was finally over.

"Tell me," Olivia invited.

"You know that we are hoping to open a new store in Chicago?"

"Hoping?" Olivia felt certain Winifred Woodward

had moved far beyond mere hopes. "I thought Sara said almost everything was nailed down?"

"It's should be." Reese spoke haltingly, obviously unaccustomed to letting others past the mask of competence he kept in place. Slowly he revealed his situation. "That location, that property—it was my idea. Grandmother had another place in mind, but I persuaded her that this property had room for everything we needed and wanted to do."

"But something's changed. I think you should tell her."

"I can't." Reese's tension was palpable.

"Because?" she probed.

"I know it's wrong to let Winifred keep planning for this project. It might never happen. But she's had a couple of minor attacks this week. Nothing serious, but it's a sign she needs to slow down." Love seeped through his words. "She's so excited, so eager to get a chapel in the place so she can share her faith. She's like a kid waiting to open a Christmas present. I'm afraid to spoil that and risk her health."

"But Reese, if it's not attainable—you can't buy the property?"

"No."

He didn't offer an explanation and Olivia didn't press for one.

"Then you have to tell her," she repeated.

"I can't. Not yet. The new store was going to fulfill so many of the goals Gran has clung to for so long.

To devastate her before I've explored every possibility is too cruel." Reese huffed out his frustration. "I've got to find a solution. That's why the family hired me."

"I'm sure it's more than that, Reese." Olivia couldn't understand this distancing of himself from his family. "They love you. They're glad you're part of the family enterprise, as your sisters are."

"Maybe." Silence, then his voice came back, stronger, more determined. "I have a couple more options to look into. If I fail—well, then I'll tell Winifred. I just hope she'll be strong enough by then. She's eighty, almost eighty-one, you know."

Though she sensed Reese wasn't telling her everything, Olivia didn't have an answer that would help him out of his situation.

"I don't know how else I can help," she told him frankly. "But I promise I will pray for you. All of you. I think Winifred's idea to bring in more of her faith is pleasing to God, and I'm certain He has a plan to make everything work out."

"That's the second time you've said that. You really believe God cares about details like this?"

"God cares about us, His children. So of course He cares about the things that trouble us, or made us sad. It's the same with you and the twins, isn't it? Well, God is no less a father than you, Reese. He always wants the best for His children. Not necessarily the easiest," she added, lest he get the wrong idea. "But the best. Who knows but this problem could lead to a solution that will make Weddings by Woodwards reach many more people."

"It's just a bridal store," Reese said, faint laughter buried in his voice.

"Some thought Paul was *just* a fisherman, too. But he spread the Good News of God's love all across his world. God uses whatever we give Him."

"That faith of yours is quite something, Olivia."

She flushed, relieved he couldn't see her face. But she refused to back down.

"It's strong," she agreed. "But it didn't get that way overnight. I had to learn to trust God. We all do. It's the only way to have a real relationship with Him. So I will pray for you to find the right solution, Reese. But I think God would like it if you talked to Him yourself."

"I can't," he grated, pain ripping out the words. "I feel like He abandoned me when He took Taylor."

"Tell Him that," Olivia urged. "Tell Him everything in your heart. He's God. He can take your anger and your pain. And He can turn them into something beautiful. If you let Him. Let him, Reese. His way is so much better."

He didn't answer. Olivia waited a moment, whispered good-night and then hung up the phone.

The moon slipped out from behind a cloud and cast its golden glow across the land. She brushed the dampness from her cheeks.

"Hold him, Father," she begged. "Show Reese Your love as You've shown me."

The night slid away as she talked to the One who understood how to put a heart back together. And finally, when peace bloomed, she went inside to prepare for another day at Byways.

She didn't expect to find the note on her windshield.

Secrets never stay secret.

Chapter Six

The ominous rumble of thunder overhead reflected the condition of Reese's stomach as he drove home from the airport.

The moment he stepped through his front door, Winifred would demand to know why he'd had to go to Chicago on a Friday. The truth was, despite his best efforts, nothing had changed. Weddings by Woodwards still had no location to open his grandmother's newest project. He'd tell her tonight.

Reese pulled into the garage and parked. After grabbing his overnight bag, he stepped inside the house. Odd that it was so quiet. Winifred loved to watch old movies in the living room and she usually did it at top volume, repeating the words along with the actors. But the only sound Reese could hear was a soft muffled rhythm that didn't resemble his grandmother's snoring at all.

A dim light illuminated the kitchen, but it was

enough to see that someone had thoroughly cleaned. The dining room was also immaculate.

"Hello?"

No answer. He prowled through the rest of the house, checking on the boys first before he scanned the other bedrooms. His grandmother was not there. Finally, in the family room, he found Olivia curled on his big sectional sofa, lightly covered by the afghan Sara had gifted to him some long-ago Christmas.

Reese paused to take in the sight.

A lamp on a nearby table cast its lambent glow over Olivia's cinnamon-red hair as it cascaded against the dark brown pillow. Her face was serene, empty of lines, her almond-tinted skin dewy soft. She did not look like a woman who had loved and lost.

Questions about Olivia had surfaced repeatedly since the day he'd met her at Sara's wedding rehearsal. Why had she come to Denver? Why did she never speak about her past? Who had she lost?

Finding those answers had become very important to him.

As he stared, her big hazel eyes flickered open and a smile drifted across her lips.

"You're home," she murmured.

In that moment Reese felt at home, something that hadn't happened once since the day he'd moved into this house. So why now? Nothing had really changed. The twins' storybooks lay helter-skelter on the armoire shelves. Toys littered the corner they played in. But not all was the same. Music, soft, almost ethereal, floated from the hidden speakers. A bouquet of dandelions filled the cut-glass vase he'd given Taylor on their first-week anniversary.

It was the same house, but different.

Because Olivia was here?

"How was your trip?" She lifted away the afghan and sat up, pushing her glossy hair off her face.

"Unproductive," Reese admitted. "Mrs. Garver is intent on selling off her assets so she can move. And the faster she can do it, the better she'll like it. We're sunk."

"I'm truly sorry."

Olivia brushed away a yawn. Only then did he realize how late it was.

"I should have been home ages ago, but the flight was delayed by a thunderstorm. It seems to have followed me."

"I stopped by with a pizza. While I was here your grandmother had a call. Apparently her doctor had an opening and insisted she take it. I volunteered to stay here so she could. I hope that was all right?"

"I'm sure the twins loved having you here, though I bet you're not the soft touch Winifred usually is. I hope she's all right."

"She didn't look ill. Perhaps a little tired."

"I shouldn't have imposed on her." Reese pushed away the guilt and sat down opposite her, enjoying the way the lamplight framed her beauty.

Olivia always looked pulled together. Reese had grown up in a house where fashion was as familiar as television sitcoms were in other homes. Though the Woodwards ate, drank and slept fashion, Reese had always preferred football and hockey. But some of their knowledge had obviously rubbed off because in Olivia's sundress Reese recognized the familiar lines of a well-known American designer.

Olivia had told him she hadn't worked for a while. But she'd just purchased an expensive new car and she was wearing designer clothes.

Who *was* she?

"No date tonight?" Hopefully she wouldn't recognize his tactics for what they were—sheer nosiness.

"I don't date."

"I'm sure the men in your life regret that."

"There are no men in my life. Unless you count Brett and Brady." Her smile defused his questions. Olivia's smile had a way of making him feel relaxed. "I'm sorry you weren't successful in Chicago. Do you have another strategy prepared?"

Though Reese was aware she'd turned the questions back on him, he was too tired to pretend he hadn't hit bottom.

"I have no idea what to do now." He explained about Mrs. Garver's need to move quickly. "It seems the harder I try, the further Gran's dream for the Chicago store recedes. I have to tell Grandmother, but—" He shook his head, refusing to go on.

"Have a little faith, Reese. God will help."

"You keep saying that, Olivia." He glared at her even as his brain protested that it wasn't her fault. "But what's changed? An old woman's dream is going to die and there's nothing I can do about it. Worse than that, it's my fault."

"How is this your fault?"

"I should have signed the lease when I had the chance."

"Without conducting due diligence? Without ensuring that everything Woodwards wanted and needed in this new property was included?" Olivia shook her head. "That would have been wrong—and totally unlike you, Reese."

"Unlike me?"

"Uh-huh. I've watched you. At Byways, with your family, with your children. You do your very best for everyone in your life. You don't skimp, you don't do things halfway and you don't quit simply because the going gets rough."

"Yeah, I'm the quintessential poster boy for duty." He was fed up with trying so hard. "Any suggestions for my next step?"

"Talk to your grandmother?"

"I will, as soon as I'm sure she's all right." He modulated his voice so as not to wake up the kids. "There's got to be something I haven't thought of. Something I haven't done."

"Your family is part of this new enterprise," Olivia insisted quietly. "If they knew, maybe they—"

"Not yet." Reese would tell no one until he'd told

Winifred, but now he'd need to be certain she was well enough to handle it. "What's been happening at Byways?"

"Nothing new." Olivia studied him then shrugged, accepting his change of subject. "Did you happen to notice Emily and Nelson?"

He remembered she'd asked him to observe the dynamics between the two.

"I haven't paid enough attention, I guess. But tomorrow is the big picnic, isn't it? I'll watch then. In the meantime, why don't you tell me what's bothering you."

"I think Nelson abuses her." Olivia met his stare head-on, nodded. "I've thought it for a while. Now I'm almost certain."

A wave of anger surged up at the thought of anyone deliberately hurting the young girl. "Are you suggesting that he hits her?"

Olivia's shaking head stopped his questions.

"It's not physical abuse, Reese, at least not yet. But I believe he does verbally abuse her. It's a kind of mental torture that makes Emily very afraid of him. She'll do anything to appease him. She's wound tight from constantly walking the tightrope of fear."

"But—" Reese hadn't expected this. "How do you know? Has she said something?"

"Exactly the opposite. I gave a talk yesterday. I explained about the many forms of abuse and how sometimes we might think we deserve it, but that no one has the right to do that." Olivia sighed. "Emily looked at her hands the entire time. She said nothing, didn't even speak to me after. In fact, even though we had a date to go for supper together, she left early."

"Olivia, missing a dinner date doesn't mean Nelson's abusing Emily." Reese didn't particularly care for the man's personality, but without some concrete proof…

"She won't say a word against her brother. I went to their house the night I took Emily home, after we had dinner here. Remember?" She waited.

Reese nodded. "Go on."

"The place is like a show home. There's no dust, not one thing out of place. I thought maybe they had a housekeeper so the other day I asked Emily if she'd recommend her to me, give me her name."

"You need a housekeeper?" Reese frowned. "I thought you live alone in a condo."

"I do, but I'm thinking of buying a house."

Nelson had been drooling over her new car. Sara envied her designer clothes. Now she was going to buy a house. What else didn't he know about Olivia Hastings?

"Listen to me, Reese. Emily said *she* is the house-keeper. She made some joke about giving herself references, but Nelson walked in and she got this look on her face, like she'd said too much, and she took off. She was terrified." Olivia dragged a hand through her hair, mussing it into glorious dishevel-ment. "I stopped by last evening to take her to a movie and she was vacuuming like there was no tomorrow. She made some excuse about Nelson hating pet hair in the house. Emily has a cat she adores, you see, but she's never allowed to let it leave her room."

"Maybe he's allergic," Reese offered, thinking how pretty Olivia looked when she was angry. The green of her eyes intensified and stood out against her pale skin and soft auburn hair. "That's not proof that she's being verbally abused."

"Not on its own, but along with everything else…" Olivia's big eyes begged him to believe her. "I've seen this before, Reese. It's what I'm trained to spot. Emily's afraid to relax or volunteer anything at Byways. She does whatever Nelson tells her to, she never argues and she won't make a move without first approving it with him. She's terribly nervous whenever he's around."

"Nelson is her guardian."

"You're the boys' guardian, but they're not afraid of you!" She moved forward, leaned toward him. "I know you don't understand why she'd stick it out if he abuses her. But you have a wonderful close-knit family who stands up for each other. Emily only has Nelson. If she doesn't do as he orders, who is left for her to turn to?"

Reese understood Emily's isolation better than Olivia could possibly imagine, though he doubted she'd believe it.

"Don't you trust my assessment of the situation?"

"Of course. You are the professional. It's your ex-

perience and judgment that Byways relies on." He
needed to be careful here. "But the kids seem to love
him. No one has a negative word about him. You
have no proof, nothing to back that assessment. The
law says I cannot even hint that Nelson is abusive
without proof. If he sued, it would shut the place
down. Other kids would never be able to use Byways.
It's too big a risk."

"So what? We let her suffer?"

"No. Of course not."

"Then what?"

"We wait, we watch and we gather evidence. I
think you should speak to Emily privately, somewhere away from Byways where there's no possibility that Nelson could overhear or break into the
conversation. Try to get her to open up."

"We can't wait forever, Reese. If Emily is in that
situation for too long, it will only make her recovery
more difficult. Her self-esteem has been severely
compromised." Olivia's voice brimmed with com-
passion. "It will take time, patience and love to
rebuild that and I don't think Emily has anyone who
can do that for her. She's alone."

Not like you. Reese could read the chastening in
her eyes.

"Then you and I will have to be her family, watch
out for her," Reese said quietly. "I care about Emily
as much as you do, Olivia."

"I know." She leaned back against the cushions,
her hazel eyes dark and stormy. "Men like Nelson are

hard to trap. They're smart and wily and they use their charm to manipulate. Don't underestimate him."

"You sound like you've had firsthand experience," Reese murmured, determined to learn more about the past she never spoke of. "When was that?"

"Social services used to refer cases to me sometimes," she said. "I ran across a variety of abusers, all of them charmers. The only way to find the truth is to look past their smooth presentation and probe underneath."

"Where was it you had these experiences?" He slid off his shoes, pretending nonchalance.

"In the east. A while ago."

Noncommittal. He tried again.

"I remember you told me you had your own practice. Did you have all ages of children or did you prefer certain cases or ages?"

"I don't care about age. I only want to help however I can." She pulled a ticket out of her pocket. "Look. Winifred invited me to the fall showing of her new collection."

Another change of subject. Reese couldn't decide whether to keep pushing or let it go. He felt like he'd shared his soul with her and yet knew very little of her past. Olivia misread his silence.

"Is it an imposition?" Her smooth forehead pleated in a frown. "I don't have to go if it's a problem. I know you and the rest of the family will be busy. I didn't expect you to—"

"Olivia."

"Yes?" She stared at him, hurt lingering in the back of her eyes.

"I'd love for you to come and see the family in action," he said simply. "Truth is, I'm usually more of a nuisance than a help at these things. They all give me jobs to do that keep me out of the way, I think because they're afraid I'll ruin something."

She rolled her eyes.

"No, it's true. I'm a good lawyer and I can usually negotiate a great contract for services rendered or draw up a rock-solid prenuptial if someone asks, current predicament notwithstanding. But I'm hopeless at almost everything fashion-oriented that goes on at Weddings by Woodwards."

"Didn't inherit any of the family genes, huh?"

"I couldn't. I was adopted. When I was four." Reese watched her eyes widen and knew he had to explain. "I thought Sara would have told you. My mother left me in their store with a note that asked the Woodwards to adopt me. So they did."

"Just like that. No questions asked?"

"Just like that," he said, smiling at her surprise. He'd often felt that way himself.

"But—why?"

"Because that's what Woodwards do," he said, repeating the phrase Winifred had used to explain it to him when he was twelve and curious. "They did investigate, asked questions, but no one had any answers. My mother was gone, no one stepped forward, so I became part of the Woodward clan and they adopted me."

"God certainly had His hand on you," Olivia murmured.

"Because I became a Woodward?" Reese needed time to consider that, but it wouldn't happen now. Olivia was speaking again.

"I can understand why you feel so strongly about disappointing your grandmother, Reese. You feel you owe her—them—and you want to repay their love. But do you realize what you're risking by keeping your secret?"

"What?" It galled him that Olivia, whom he was sure would understand, didn't.

"You're risking alienating them. They love you, Reese," she said, her tone serious. "They've proven that over and over by including you, by making you a member of the family, by drawing you into the business. Don't you think it's going to hurt when they realize that you kept this from them, that you didn't allow them to help?"

"You don't understand."

"Then explain it."

Reese inhaled, filling his lungs with oxygen as he searched for a way to begin. But there was no way to express his silly, childish feelings without blurting out the whole mess.

"Olivia, I need to figure this out on my own."

"Because?"

"Because I've always been the needy one. I'm the

penniless no-name kid who shares their bounty. It's my duty to prove I'm worth the trust they put in me, that I'm worthy of being a Woodward."

Olivia stared at him for several minutes before flopping backward against the sofa cushions.

"I've never heard anything so stupid in my entire life," she sputtered.

"Thanks." Reese felt like an idiot.

"Sorry. That didn't come out right." She made a funny face at him, grimaced. "I'll try again."

"Don't bother. It's late, you're tired. So am I. I appreciate you taking over for Winifred. I shouldn't have expected her to look after the twins. They take too much out of her. But I was desperate to make that flight." Reese rose, kept talking, anything to avoid that pitying look on Olivia's face. "I guess I'll see you at the picnic tomorrow."

"Shut up, Reese."

He blinked, grinned.

"That's a no-no word in this house," he told her, tongue in cheek.

Olivia blushed.

"Sorry, but will you please sit down and let me explain what I meant."

"No need. You're free to hold any opinion you want."

"Reese."

He recognized the tone. Firm. No-nonsense. No room for argument. Olivia was a lot like Winifred.

Reese sat.

"First of all, I apologize. I shouldn't have said what I did." A tiny smile kicked up the corners of her mouth. "It's just that sometimes your logic stuns me."

"What logic?" He didn't like where this was heading.

"Whatever logic tells you that you can earn love, that you can actually do something to be worthy of being a Woodward." She shook her head. "I understand that you feel indebted, that you'd like to repay them. But isn't their love a debt that is not repayable? How much is enough to repay someone for loving you?"

"I wasn't exactly trying to repay—" He had been. "I don't want to crush Winifred's dream. She's planned this for a long time, and I admit, I've been encouraging her as much as anyone. To have to cancel the store now, when we're so close—it's not going to be easy."

"See, that's the part I have trouble with." Olivia glared at him. "How do you *know* you have to cancel? Because *you* haven't come up with a plan? If you'd talk to your family, let them in on the problem—"

"Not yet. My parents are trying to sort through some production problems that could wreak havoc with the autumn line. Sara's busy with another makeup class for burn victims, not to mention her new husband and taking over for Katie, who is working overtime in accounts to try and collect some past-due bills to improve our cash flow. And my brother, Donovan, is still overseas. Everyone's maxed out." Reese hoped she understood that he simply had to find a way himself.

"You're very stubborn." Olivia's smile never stayed hidden for long. "Okay, have it your way. For now. But I'm not giving up on this."

"I never thought you would. *Bulldog* is a descriptor that comes to mind."

"Look in the mirror, pal." But she grinned good-naturedly. "At least promise you'll talk to me. I'm no lawyer, but I get the odd idea that sometimes works out."

"You've certainly had your share of them at Byways." Olivia was smart and generous and willing to let him vent. And Reese didn't want her to go home yet. "Would you like some iced tea? Chicago was boiling and I'm parched."

"Sure." She rose and followed him into the kitchen, her bare feet padding on the tile.

As Olivia walked past him and perched on one of the counter stools, he caught a hint of her fragrance. Very feminine, flowery, with a hint of spice. It suited her.

"Lemon pie?" Reese held on to the fridge door as he turned to study her. "Grandmother doesn't make lemon pie."

"I did. I also made an apple one and a peach one. They're in the freezer." She grinned, shrugged. "I was bored, and this kitchen is very tempting."

"I've never had any problem with it." He cut himself a huge piece and, when she declined, returned the pie to the fridge. "I should ask you to sit with the twins more often."

"I wouldn't mind. Those two don't have to work very hard to worm their way into my heart." Olivia watched him take the first bite, smiled as he closed his eyes to savor the pie.

"It seems like we're always having tea in here," he said, following her with his eyes as she rinsed the teapot, added two bags and filled it with boiling water. "If anyone saw us, they'd think we were in our dotage."

"You don't have to be old to enjoy tea, Reese Woodward." Olivia smacked two mugs on the counter and pretended to glare. "I drink it all the time."

"I know," he said. "I've seen you. It seems to be all you drink. And I've been meaning to ask—what's wrong with coffee?"

Her hands froze midair and she stared at him, her big eyes round with surprise. Then, with no warning, tears began coursing down her cheeks.

"Olivia, please. I'm sorry. What did I say?" Reese jumped forward, feeling utterly helpless, wondering how he'd brought on this deluge. He reached out and caught a teardrop on the tip of his finger. "Olivia?"

When she didn't move away, he slipped his arms around her and drew her close.

"I'm so sorry I upset you. Please tell me what's wrong," he begged as he held her.

"I never cry." But her tears kept falling.

"I know. You're tough and invincible and you're there for everyone. But even you have to weaken once in a while. Guess I'm not the only one who needs to talk, huh?" Reese smiled as Olivia tucked her head against his chest to avoid looking at him. The move reminded him of the twins when they were embarrassed by their tears. "I've heard talking about things sometimes helps."

She lifted her head, gave him a droll look.

"I'm sure a very wise person told you that."

"Yes, she is. Very wise."

Olivia visibly gathered her composure, swiping her palms across her cheeks as she pressed away the dampness. A sniff or two and strong, invincible Dr. Hastings was back.

"Don't look so scared, Reese," she teased. She eased herself out of his arms. "I'm over it. I almost never do that."

"If you could tell me what I did to bring it on this time, I'd promise never do it again," he promised fervently.

"It wasn't you. It was just—someone I knew used to say that all the time. 'What's wrong with coffee?'" Her voice wobbled for an instant and a watery smile hovered. "He always teased me about drinking tea."

"He was special, wasn't he? Someone you cared about? Someone you lost?"

Olivia nodded, her drenched green gaze filled with the past.

"He could make everything fun," she murmured. "If he had his coffee. Tea never gave Trevor the boost he liked and he wouldn't let me forget it. You reminded me of him just now."

"You miss him. I'm sorry, Olivia. I know how difficult it is sometimes when the memories swamp you."

"Yes." Her face radiated a soft pink glow that made her look young and innocent and so sweet. "But they're good memories. Trevor was a wonderful man."

Whom she'd loved. He knew that from the tone of her voice.

"I'm fine now."

"Good. I, Reese Woodward, promise never to speak of coffee again," he promised, holding his left hand up as if taking a pledge. "Though there were parts of your tear-storm I quite enjoyed." He grinned at her deepening blush. "Would you like some tea, Olivia?"

"Yes, I would. Thank you."

They drank it on the back deck, watching clouds scud across the sky. In the distance, electric white bolts speared the darkness accompanied by murmuring undertones of thunder.

"It's going to storm." Reese glanced at Olivia and found her staring at him.

"Are you afraid of storms?" she asked, her voice hushed and solemn.

"No. Are you?"

"Sometimes. Storms signal change and change is hard for me."

Reese had a thousand questions, but he asked only one.

"Why?"

"Because when you've lost someone you loved, it's hard to let yourself care again."

And with that cryptic comment Olivia rose, found her purse and left so quickly Reese barely had time to say good-night.

As the storm moved in, Reese knew he needed to learn more about Olivia Hastings.

Somehow.

Chapter Seven

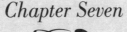

Byways Picnic Day turned into a blast.

Olivia couldn't stop giving thanks for the gorgeous weather, family attendance and general cooperation.

The only fly in the ointment, of course, was Nelson.

"Barbecue? For this herd?" His scoffing smile required no translation.

"Yes. Now can you get the briquettes going or not?" Olivia was fed up with trying to coax Nelson out of his perpetual bad mood. "Shall I find someone else?"

"Find someone else for what?" Reese stood in the doorway to the kitchen, a twin on either side.

"To help with a crazy barbecue idea. I understood we'd agreed to serve sandwiches, but Olivia seems to think we can cook hamburgers fast enough to feed everyone who's shown up today. Thing is, we never imagined such a large turnout."

"I did. I expected all of them," Olivia said quietly.

"I've been hoping and praying they'd want to know what their children have been doing, why they're so excited about Byways. The attendance today is proof that Byways has become a kind of community drawing point. But we need to feed them. I thought a barbecue would be fun. That's why I cleaned up that massive great grill that was sitting out back."

She waited for Nelson's refusal. Instead Reese spoke.

"If you don't want to the light the briquettes, I can ask one of the board members to do it, Nelson. I'm not yet finished judging the kite flying. We came for a bathroom break." Reese lifted an eyebrow of inquiry. "Or I'll do it and you can fill in for me."

"I'll take your place. I hate the mess those briquettes make." With a sour glance at Olivia, Nelson left.

"He's got a point about the mess," Olivia pointed out. She hunkered down on a level with the twins. "While your daddy's busy, would you two like to help me in the kitchen?"

"Yes!"

Bathroom break over, Reese laid out the rules for the twins and with a skeptical look at Olivia, left via the back stairs to go outside and grill. The twins eagerly laid out plates on one of the long tables where she'd placed a huge cake.

"Are we cele-cel-brat—" Brady looked to his brother, but Brett offered no help.

"Celebrating," Olivia enunciated. "Yes, I guess we are."

"Why?"

"Because we all enjoy coming to Byways to have fun." She glanced down the table. Brett seemed spellbound by the size of the cake. "Do you like it?" she asked him.

"I'm gonna ask Daddy if Brady 'n' me can have a cake this big for our birthday," he said, his brown eyes enormous.

A noise in the doorway made Olivia look up. Reese stood watching his son.

"That's a good idea, son. Olivia, would you mind helping with their birthday party?" He told her the date. The twins added their pleas.

"I'll be happy to help. But Brett, I thought your dad would make monster mash pie for your birthdays," she said tongue in cheek as she grinned at Reese.

"Monster pies aren't for birthdays," Brett scoffed. "'Sides, Daddy always lets us pick out a cake at the bakery. I like black."

"Hence your grubby T-shirt," Reese teased. He grinned at Olivia. "Briquettes lit. Give 'em half an hour or so and they'll be ready to cook."

"Perfect." Emily stood hovering behind Reese so Olivia beckoned. "C'mon, Emily. I'm about to cut open some buns. You could put out the ketchup and mustard if you'd like."

She gave them all tasks, as well as the various

parents and Byways workers who came to offer assistance. In a short time everything lay ready and waiting. Emily had been folding napkins with the twins. Suddenly she jumped to her feet, knocking her chair backward so it rattled against the cement floor in a loud crash.

"I forgot," she gasped. "Nelson said I'm supposed to be a marker for the ball throw."

"I want to go, too," Brett yelled, grabbing her arm.

"No, Brett!" Emily, her face bleached of all color, jerked away from the boy and dashed across the room. Her footsteps pounded up the stairs and the door banged loudly.

"I want to go help Emily, Daddy," Brett whined.

Reese looked at Olivia, eyes narrowed.

"I don't think she needs help right now, son. But if Olivia doesn't need us, maybe we'll go watch the ball throw for a little while." He waited for her assent.

"Of course. Go. We have everything well in hand here." *Watch the interaction between brother and sister,* Olivia wanted to add. But she didn't.

"Okay. See you later. Come on, Brady."

The rest of the day passed in a whirl of activity and Olivia never got a chance to speak with Reese again until the last straggler had left the building and she was in her office, typing out a report of the day's activities.

"Why is it you look as fresh as you did this morning and I'm filthy and worn out?" Reese demanded, leaning against the door frame.

"Clean living," she shot back, rubbing her tired toes against the worn carpeting beneath her desk. "Where are the twins?"

"Emily's reading them a story on the front steps. Bedtime's going to be a breeze." Reese moved forward, sank into the chair she kept for visitors. "Emily's willing to babysit tonight. Are you interested in going for dinner with me to some place that does not serve hamburgers or hot dogs and especially cake with black icing?"

She had a hunch he was going to hold that icing against her for a while.

"It wasn't that bad. A few dots here and there." Olivia murmured, procrastinating.

It sounded like a date and she was hesitant to get romantically involved right now. Whoever had left that note was watching her. It could be a reporter who would love to write a story about her dating again. But Olivia wanted to find out how much Reese had noticed today. Her worries about Emily were growing faster than the dandelions in the flower bed that the twins insisted on watering every time they visited.

"Hey, I didn't realize you'd have such a hard time deciding. You're hard on the ego, lady." Reese made a face. "Do I have to use the boys to coax you to come? I warn you, that means pizza and noise. Lots of noise."

She giggled.

"I'd love to have dinner with you," she said and

realized it was true. With Reese she didn't feel all the awkwardness that came with dating someone. And why would she? They were just friends. There wasn't anything romantic between them. "But I'd really like to have a shower first."

"I know the feeling." He plucked his red-stained shirt away from his chest. "Why does the food industry choose to make drinks in such vivid colors?"

"You could have given them water." She chuckled. "Where shall I meet you?"

"I could pick you up. Or not." Reese hurried out to intervene in the twins' argument before returning to name the restaurant. "Seven-thirty?"

"I'll be there."

Reese almost made it across the parking lot, but ran into Nelson on the way to his car.

"Hey, Nelson. Emily said she okayed it with you to babysit tonight. Is there a problem?"

"I have no problem. She's making good money off of you."

Reese disliked Nelson's smarmy smile.

"Emily deserves her wages. She works hard with the kids." He waited, but Nelson didn't say anything more. "So, I guess we'll see you later, then. That is, if you'll be there when I bring Emily home." He tried not to make it sound like a question.

"No, I won't. I have a lot of cleanup to do here. Olivia says she's going out again and can't stay late."

His eyes widened. He pretended surprise. "Oh, she's going out with you."

Reese glanced around the property.

"There shouldn't be that much to do. The board members made sure things were shipshape before they left."

"They did a great job," Nelson said. "Really great. But there are always a few things that only people who work here recognize as out of place. I'll handle it. I'm used to doing it."

Alone. That was the implication.

Reese tracked his gaze to the side stairs. Olivia descended with her laptop and purse. Her car sat nearby. He lifted a hand and waved. It seemed a long time before Olivia waved back. She deposited her belongings inside her shiny new vehicle, then hurried back inside the building.

"She's an interesting woman," Nelson said, his voice filled with innuendo.

"She's certainly worked hard for Byways. You all have," Reese added lest he offend the activities director. "All afternoon the kids have been telling me how you or she has been there when you were needed. Things seem to be working out well between you and Olivia."

"I guess." Nelson glanced at Emily, who was playing a game of tag nearby. Reese noted the way the man's eyes hardened as he watched her. "Olivia has an aura of mystery around her, don't you think?"

"Mystery?" Reese frowned. "I hadn't noticed."

"I'm sure you're more observant than that. Take Olivia's car, for instance. It's an expensive model. I wonder how she affords it. I know I have to be frugal to make the payments on my secondhand one and I've been working for years. This is the first job Olivia's had in a while, apparently."

"Nelson, I don't know anything about her financial—"

"She paid for that cake out of her own pocket, too. A massive cake like that must have cost a lot. And her clothes." He sucked air between his teeth in a manner that suggested something amiss.

Reese didn't like where this was heading, but he wasn't sure how to head Nelson off. Maybe it was better to listen and learn.

"What's wrong with her clothes?"

"Nothing's *wrong* with them. They're all top-of-the-line. Did you notice her bag?" Nelson named a designer. "Four hundred dollars! I should know. Emily's been admiring it so much I checked to see if I could get one for her birthday gift. But that's way out of my league."

"Maybe Olivia got it for her birthday. Look, I really need to get going."

"Yes, of course. Will Emily be very late?" Nelson's mincing tone intimated that Reese often kept his sister out past midnight.

"I wouldn't think so. What time do you want her home?" And wasn't that tossing the ball back into Nelson's corner?

"I'm not trying to be nasty, but Reese, you're a parent. You know how it is." Nelson smiled at him as if they shared a heavy duty. "You try to do all the right things, don't you?"

"Uh—"

"Same with me. I like to have an idea of when my sister will be home. Olivia insists on picking her up for church on Sunday mornings. Sometimes all poor Emily can do is drag herself out of bed. She comes home so tired she has to retire early to catch up on her sleep."

Retire early? A thirteen-year-old girl?

"Don't worry. She'll be home early tonight." Reese's jaw ached from clenching it. Restraint hurt. He called the twins and Emily to get in the car, anxious to get out of here before he blurted out something he'd regret. "See you later, Nelson."

"Yes. Have a good time, Emily."

Reese assessed the smile Nelson gave his little sister and the way she responded. *Foreboding* was the best descriptor he could come up with.

They drove home singing silly songs. As soon as Reese opened the front door, the twins raced through the house toward the trampoline. Reese insisted they wait for Emily before they climbed on.

"She'll be out in a minute. I need to talk to her first."

As Emily watched the twins leave, fear flooded her face.

"Did I do something wrong?"

"Of course not. I just wanted to thank you for babysitting tonight. I hope you didn't have other plans. I don't want you to always give them up for us if you do. You deserve your free time, too."

"I didn't have any plans."

"Really? Great. Then it worked out." Reese smiled as he asked the question that had nagged him all the way home. "Do you like going to church with Olivia? Nelson said she picks you up on Sunday mornings."

"I love it." Pure joy flooded her freckled face. "There's a man who plays the guitar—he's awesome. I'm saving up so I can get some lessons from him."

"Do you have a guitar?"

"No." Her joy leached away. "Olivia said she'd help me find a place where I can rent one when I've saved enough."

"There's a guitar in the garage. My brother, Donovan, tried to teach me to play, but he's been overseas for several years and I've forgotten everything. You're welcome to learn on that guitar. If you want to, of course."

"I'd love it. Thank you." Emily wrapped her thin arms around his waist in a rush of exuberance, then quickly backed away. "Oh, s-sorry," she stammered.

"No, problem." Reese grinned at her. "Do you want me to get it now?"

"Maybe later. I need to look after the twins." But she cast one longing look at the door that led to the garage.

"The twins will go to bed soon. Then you can practice all you like. I'll go get it while you look after them on the trampoline."

"Okay." She hurried away. A few minutes later her laughter rang out.

By the time he'd found Donovan's guitar and the few instruction books he'd used, Reese was filthy. He was also going to be late.

"I should have allowed more time," he muttered as he dusted himself off. He tried Olivia's home number but no one answered.

"I'll call her cell. You go and have your shower," Emily insisted. "I'll bathe them while you change, then we'll make some sandwiches for dinner."

"You're a peach." He ruffled her hair then took the stairs two at a time.

Even with Emily's help, Reese arrived at the restaurant half an hour late.

"I'm very sorry," he muttered as he slid into his seat in the booth he'd reserved, a favorite seat that overlooked the South Platte River. "Are you starved?"

"No. I ordered some hors d'oeuvres." Olivia looked cool and elegant in a navy silk sundress. This one emphasized her long, slender neck and shapely arms. "Try some," she invited, pushing the plate toward him.

"Rabbit food." Reese popped one bite of cauliflower into his mouth and crunched it into oblivion. "That isn't going to last me very long. I'm starved."

"Let's order, then."

Reese scorned her choice of fish so Olivia regaled him with health warnings about too much red meat. That led to a discussion of the afternoon's menu and of course, to Nelson.

"He seemed better today. Or was that my imagination?" he asked, admiring her beauty in the soft candle glow from their table.

Olivia had piled her hair on the top of her head and left just a few wisps loose. They caressed her cheeks in the gentle breeze that blew off the river. Faceted stones glimmered like stars in her earlobes. Diamonds?

"Nelson is always better when the board is around." Olivia lifted her lashes to meet his stare. She smiled. "Don't take this the wrong way, Reese, but could we please not talk about Nelson tonight?"

"Sure." He leaned back, delighted by the prospect of learning more about her. "What were you like as a little girl?"

"Spoiled rotten." Olivia relaxed against the banquette and tipped her head, allowing him to see her self-satisfied smirk. "I had a perfect childhood. I wanted for nothing. I was loved, and I knew it."

"Sounds ideal."

"It was." A wistful edge clung to her smile. "My parents died when I was six. My grandfather raised me. I grew up outside a little town where being his granddaughter was a ticket to freedom. Gramps's friends were his cronies from his job. They talked about everything. I'd sneak downstairs and fall asleep listening to them."

"He's gone now?" Reese wished he hadn't asked when her face saddened.

"I miss him every day. He was the most sensible, most generous, most solid parent a girl could have had. He helped me learn so many things." A half smile lifted her lips. "Gramps taught me to love God."

Reese had figured as much. But he didn't interrupt. This was more information than Olivia had ever given about herself. He wanted to know more.

"You remind me of him a little, Reese."

"Me? Of your grandfather?" Oh, great. Every man's dream was to remind a gorgeous woman of her grandfather. "How?"

"The whole due diligence thing."

She'd said that before.

"Meaning?"

"Well." Olivia swirled her fingertip on an ice cube while she thought. When she looked at him, her hazel eyes darkened. "Gramps never did anything halfway. If he was going to do it, he checked out all the pros and cons and decided his course. Then he stuck to it. Everything he did, he did well."

"Very flattering. Thank you."

"You're welcome." She chuckled, the sound a musical tone in the intimacy of the dim restaurant.

"Where did you live?"

"Gramps always wanted to be a farmer. He bought

an acreage in Wisconsin just before my parents died. I had chickens, a lamb, a cow and a horse. I had two dogs, Gingersnap and Chocolate Chip." She grinned. "I'd forgotten about them."

"The twins are always after me to get them a dog." Reese groaned at her look. "Don't you start. I can barely manage two little boys. Adding a puppy to the mix makes me shake with fear. The mess would be catastrophic."

"It wouldn't have to be a puppy. My dau—" She choked off the rest, took a sip of water. "You could get an older animal that was gentle."

"No dogs, please," Reese pleaded and only half in jest. What had she been going to say? "Not till I master being a single parent."

"Do you think one ever masters being a parent? A child changes and grows as they experience life. All you can do is be there, offer your shoulder or your lap and make sure they feel secure." Olivia's sadness turned inward. "I always felt safe with my grandfather."

"Don't you feel safe now?" He wondered what made her survey the room so frequently. "Olivia, is something wrong?"

"No." She blinked, sat up straight and refocused. "Of course not. But if there was, my protector is God. He won't let anything happen to me." She gazed out the window. "Living in Denver is kind of like living in God's shadow, you know. That's one of the reasons I moved here."

"Huh?"

"That must sound weird." She smiled at his puzzled look. "Many of the Psalms talk about David hiding in the mountains and talking to God. When I first came here, those Rockies seemed to hug the city like a mantle of protection, just as David described."

"Oh." Was the Bible that real to her? And why would she need protection? Reese had a thousand questions, but Olivia had her own.

"What was it like, when you first came to live with the Woodwards?"

"Like moving to another planet. There was always someone around." The strangeness of those days still haunted him. "Fiona likes harmony. She was constantly checking to see if I needed something. Thomas never stopped encouraging me. Winifred didn't distinguish between me and Sara or Donovan or Katie. I was her grandchild from the moment I walked into that house."

"You sound surprised."

"I guess I am."

"Even after all these years?" She laid down her fork and studied him, her head tilted to one side like a curious bird.

"It still stuns me, the way they just swept me up, no questions asked."

"Is that why you feel you have to earn their love?"

Reese was spared answering immediately because their server came to remove their dishes. Olivia ordered a slice of key lime pie and he went for the chocolate cake.

"Should I ask a different question?" Olivia cute smile teased. "I'd really like to know, but I don't want to press or embarrass you."

"Tell you what," he bargained, seeing his chance. "I'll answer your question if you'll answer mine."

Fear filled her eyes though she quickly blinked it away.

"I have nothing to hide."

Judging by her reaction, Reese was fairly certain that wasn't true. But he pretended otherwise.

"I have a hard time trusting people," he admitted, playing with his spoon. "Maybe it's because of my childhood, maybe I'm not the trusting type. Or maybe I carry a chip around on my shoulder. Taylor accused me of that once." The memory made him chuckle.

"What was she like—your Taylor?"

Normally Reese would have changed the subject, but with Olivia it seemed perfectly natural to reveal memories he usually kept tucked under his heart.

"She was stubborn as a mule and as gentle as a butterfly. She never did anything halfway." He looked at Olivia and told the truth. "She had faith like yours. Unstoppable. I thought she'd always be there. It was like God played a dirty trick when the police arrived that night to tell me she'd been killed. If it weren't for the boys—" He refused to finish that. "Anyway, after that it seemed impossible for me to trust God. It still does."

"Because He doesn't play by your rule book?" Olivia touched his hand, her fingers smooth and delicate against his skin, as they had been that night at his house. Reese wanted to grab them and hang on. But that would be taking the easy way out.

He'd tried to ride on the coattails of Taylor's faith and that hadn't worked. He didn't intend to repeat the mistake.

"Maybe. I answered your question," he murmured. "Will you answer mine?"

"What is it?"

Reese hesitated. But he couldn't deny himself this opportunity. "Where was your last practice?"

"My own? New York." The words fell so quietly he had to lean in to hear. "But that was a while ago. I had to—take some time off."

"Why?"

"Personal reasons." Olivia stared straight at him, but she did not elaborate.

Their desserts arrived, but neither of them seemed to have much appetite. Olivia asked for containers to take them home and once everything was packed up, she gathered up her white shawl and led the way to the parking lot.

"Thank you for a very nice dinner."

She looked small and defenseless, and Reese didn't want to leave her. Not yet. But he couldn't suggest going to her place, and if they went to his, there was a chance the twins might interrupt their talk. His cell phone rang.

Reese listened for a moment then agreed to come immediately.

"There's been a break-in at Byways," he explained. "They can't reach Nelson, and apparently your cell isn't on. I need to go and make sure everything is okay."

"I'll follow you."

They arrived twenty minutes later. Two policemen were on the scene.

"The thieves appear to have been interested in just one office. This one." The officer pointed to Olivia's office. "You'll need a new door and lock."

As he turned from surveying the damage, Reese caught the flash of panic Olivia tried to hide.

"It's all right," he murmured, setting his arm around her shoulder. "We'll get it repaired. Our insurance will replace whatever they took."

"It's not what they took," she whispered. "Look." She pointed to her Rolodex.

Reese could see someone had removed a number of the address cards, flicked through them, then tossed them aside to scatter around the room.

"They were looking for something specific," she whispered.

"Any idea what?"

"Not really." But she didn't look at him.

Reese was left wondering what address Olivia Hastings had that a thief would risk breaking into an alarmed building to get? And why.

He wanted answers from Olivia, and soon.

Chapter Eight

"The house is yours. Possession date in two weeks."

Friday was starting off just right.

"Thank you," Olivia breathed. "Thank you very much." She hung up the phone before sending a grateful prayer to the Father who knew her deepest yearnings.

"Olivia?" Nelson stood in the doorway, impatience written all over his face. "Are you sick?"

"No. Just tired. Does it get this hot in Denver every year?"

"Why? Going to ditch Byways for cooler climes?" It didn't sound like a joke and the look on Nelson's face told her he wasn't teasing.

"Did you need something special?" She whispered yet another prayer for patience to deal with him the way God would. "I've got an appointment at the bank."

"Yeah, I heard you were buying a house. Congrats."

"Thanks." Olivia lifted an eyebrow in reminder.

"Casey took a message for you. At least I think it's for you. Casey said the woman asked for Olivia. The last name was jumbled, but Casey assumed it was you she wanted because there's only one Olivia here. Since Casey had to leave I promised I'd pass it on. A Nancy Paret?" He held out the pink slip of paper, his eyes scrutinizing her.

"Thanks." Olivia fought to keep her face expressionless as she reached out to grasp the paper. She studied Casey's untidy scrawl. "Yeah, that's me. Nancy's a friend. I'll call her in the morning."

"I see." Nelson's thin merciless lips twisted. "What name would she be calling you by?"

"Hard to say. Nancy's a teaser." Olivia said no more. He would twist it anyway. But every single nerve in her body was wound so tight she thought she'd crack. She stuffed the note in her pocket, gathered up her purse and laptop and headed for the door.

"See you tomorrow, Nelson. Don't forget to lock up."

"Yeah. Sure, Olivia-whoever-you-are."

When she finally reached her car, Olivia slid inside, started the engine and air-conditioning then rested her aching head on the steering wheel.

She'd warned Nancy so often. It must be important for her to call Byways, but Olivia wasn't going to call back until she was safely at home. In the meantime…

"Oh, Lord, You are my rock and my shield. You are my protection. Hide me in the security of Your love. Give me strength and wisdom."

She prayed until her heart eased and her soul felt bathed in peace. Then she shifted gears and drove over to look at her new home, stuffing the past and all the stress and pain that came with it to the very back of her mind as she repeated the verse she'd chosen as her life's verse four years ago.

For the Holy Sprit, God's gift, doesn't want you to be afraid of people, but to be wise and strong and to love them and enjoy being with them.

Reese gripped his cell phone.

Measles at playschool. Exactly what he needed.

"Hi, Grandmother. It's Reese. I'm in trouble. Again." He laid out his problem. "I can't miss the Byways board meeting this afternoon because I'm to present the quotes of the structural work we want to do."

"I remember when you and your siblings had measles." Winifred chuckled, her voice slightly hoarse. "You all looked ridiculous."

"If I recall, you took pictures to taunt us with." Having Winifred as a grandmother and boss was both a challenge and a delight. Reese chuckled. "I remember having to pay you to get mine."

"Did I tell you I kept the negatives?" She laughed at his groan. "You never know when you might need blackmail like that."

"Grandmother!"

"Scared, huh?"

Reese wondered at the pause in the conversation. She'd been out of the office twice this week, but he hadn't been able to find out why. He'd assumed she was sick, but didn't ask. Winifred hated the family fussing over her health.

Just for a moment Reese wondered if the tests his father had spoken of had gone all right. But Thomas would have told him if anything was wrong with Winifred.

"I've fed and bathed the boys. They're ready for bed. Are you sure—"

"I *had* a cold. I'm fine," Winifred insisted. "Besides, Sara and Cade are here. They'll help tuck them in. They can stay over tonight. That will give you time to prepare tomorrow morning. But stop by on your way home because I want to talk to you."

Uh-oh. That sounded ominous. Reese thanked her and headed towards Byways. Hopefully he'd only be a few minutes late.

While parking in his usual spot near the door, Reese spotted Nelson talking to some kids, but as soon as they spotted him, they hurried away. Curious.

"Hey, Reese. Got the figures together?"

"Yes. Is everyone inside?"

"I'm just going in. Olivia's on the phone. Strangest thing," Nelson murmured, stroking the goatee on his chin. It was such an affectation, Reese wanted to laugh, but the look on Nelson's face stopped him.

"What's strange about a phone call?"

"Usually nothing. But yesterday this woman phoned and called Olivia by another name. Casey and I thought she had the wrong person, but Olivia recognized the caller, said she's a friend. Why would she use another name?"

"No idea, Nelson. Can you give me a hand getting this stuff inside?"

"Sure."

The meeting was in progress when Olivia slipped into one of the seats at the back of the room. Because of the Chicago situation and Winifred's cold, which had kept her out of the office, Reese had been bogged down at work and hadn't seen Olivia for two weeks. Well, not counting the Sunday service he'd taken the boys to. Olivia had been there for that, but she'd been sitting in front and probably never noticed him rush away after the last prayer.

"So those are the quotes. I move we take a couple of weeks to think things over, figure out if we want to go ahead and meet again when we've all had time to study everything." Reese waited as the motion was passed. "Any other business? Okay, meeting adjourned."

"Quick meeting," Olivia said, watching as he packed his briefcase.

"Well, it's not a regularly scheduled one and since we're all busy I figured there was no need to keep everyone late. How are you? I heard you'd bought a house."

"Emily," she guessed, smiling. "Yes, I did. I'm moving in soon. Then I'll really feel at home."

"Has it been a while since you lived in your own place?" he asked.

Her smile faded.

"Too long."

"Well, I hope you don't think me rude, but I've had a summons from Winifred and I better get over there. Have a good weekend."

"Thanks. See you."

The pull of attraction was every bit as strong as it had been last time, and Reese found it hard to walk away from Olivia. He put his things in the car and then, before he could second guess himself, went back inside Byways to offer his help during her moving day.

"Back again?" Nelson asked.

"Forgot to tell Olivia something. Is she still downstairs?"

Nelson shook his head.

"That woman called again. I think Olivia's in her office. Sure seems like a lot of cloak-and-dagger stuff."

Nelson's innuendos and negative intimations about Olivia were wearing thin. Reese couldn't imagine how she put up with it day after day. He walked toward her office, hand up to rap on the door. But it was partway open and she was speaking to someone.

"Nancy, please remember to call me Hastings.

Otherwise a lot of people are going to start asking questions that I don't want to answer."

Shock hit Reese like a tidal wave. Nelson was right. Olivia was hiding something. Like who she really was, for one thing.

Reeling from betrayal, Reese walked outside, climbed in his car and drove toward his grandmother's. He'd trusted Olivia, fallen for her claim to deep, pure faith. He'd believed she was as innocent as she seemed. He'd even been willing to believe there was nothing wrong with her refusal to talk about the past. But using a different name—how could there be anything good in that?

Reese sat in Winifred's driveway for several minutes, struggling to wrap his brain around it. Finally he grabbed his phone and dialed.

"You did some research for Byways a while ago. The subject was Olivia Hastings. Can you read me the report again?"

He listened to the few facts, the clean criminal check and the lack of anything negative.

"Can you do another search and dig deeper this time? I want to know whatever you can find, as soon as you can. Thanks."

Then Reese closed his phone, got out of the car and knocked on Winifred's door. Olivia had told him he could trust God. How could he now that it seemed Olivia was a fraud?

"Reese? What's wrong? You look horrible. Come in." Winifred tugged on his arm, coughing slightly at the extra exertion. "Don't let the door slam. The boys are asleep, and I need to talk to you undisturbed."

"Grandmother, I really need a cup of coffee. Can we go to the kitchen for this?"

His diminutive grandmother led the way in her heels and silk dress. Nothing in her demeanor showed any sign of dishevelment. Of course she'd perfected babysitting long ago, but when she swayed and clasped the door frame, he rushed to her side.

"Okay?"

"Fine. The doctor keeps changing my pills, and it makes me dizzy." She moved away to begin making coffee.

"I'm sure coffee isn't what you need to drink right now." Reese inhaled the rich fragrant brew, thinking of Olivia's reaction not long ago. "What did you want to talk about?"

"Chicago. I'm hearing rumors, Reese. Lots of rumors. Such as the future of that store may be in jeopardy. I want to know why you haven't told me." Her piercing eyes dared him to talk his way out of it, but her tiny body looked too frail to withstand the truth.

When she suddenly sank into a chair and clasped a hand to her chest, Reese knew he'd have to sugarcoat it.

"Calm down, Grandmother. There have been some problems. I'm working on the solution."

"I want to know all—the truth," she whispered, but her face was pale.

"I've had some trouble with the lease. You can trust me to handle it."

"Like you trust me enough to tell me the truth?" she snapped, her temper rushing back.

That encouraged Reese more than anything. Winifred was a fighter.

"Grandmother." He smiled, lowered his voice. "You're not feeling well and if you tell the truth, you haven't been for a while. You owe it to yourself to do what the doctors say and let the rest of us carry the load for a while."

"But—"

Reese rested his finger over her lips then bent and brushed her brow with his lips. He poured her a cool drink and helped her sip it for a few moments until some color had returned to her cheeks.

"You entrusted me to do this job and I'm trying. There are issues about the property because the owner passed away, but I'm handling that. I'm doing my very best for your company, Grandmother. Can't you trust me?"

"You'll tell me if and when you need help, is that understood?"

"Yes, ma'am."

She studied him for a moment, patted his cheek and sighed.

"All right then, son. I'll depend on you."

Relief filled Reese that she'd finally stopped worrying about the subject, but Winifred wasn't quite finished.

"I don't know what makes you such a loner, Reese." Her quiet, reflective tone held a hint of hurt. "I've tried for years to understand why you can't relax and let yourself be a part of this family instead of always trying to prove yourself to us."

"I don't—"

"You do. And let me finish." Winifred's smooth forehead wrinkled. "We are your family, Reese. We love you and we will continue to support and care about you no matter what happens. Do you understand that?"

"Yes, Grandmother." He kissed the top of her head. "I love you, too."

"You don't want to tell me anything else?"

"No. I want you to rest and forget about the company for a while." He waited, holding her gaze until her sigh told him she'd let it go for now. "I want you back in good health. Otherwise I won't let you sit the twins again." He glanced over her head into the TV room. "I'm taking them home so you can relax."

"Wait. I want to talk to you about something else." Winifred was seldom at a loss for words, but at the moment she seemed to search for the right ones. "What else is wrong?"

"What do you mean?" Reese fingered his cell phone, trying to figure out how to call Fiona without Winifred knowing.

"You roared into my driveway as if you had a fire in the backseat, then you were talking on the phone

and waving your hand. After that you just sat there.
I want to know what's wrong, and don't brush me
off."

No point in prevaricating. That would only worry
her further.

"It's Olivia."

Winifred nodded her silver head as if she'd
expected that. "Go on."

"Olivia Hastings. Or whatever her name is."

"What does that mean?"

Reese explained Nelson's insinuations and what
he'd overheard.

"All this time she's been lying."

"Why do you say that? Didn't you do a check on
her that turned up nothing?" She waited for his nod.
"So? Lots of people change their names. It's entirely
possible that Olivia did, too, but I fail to see anything
criminal in that."

"Grandmother, you're too—"

"If you say *sweet,* I'll pull your ear," Winifred
snapped. "Olivia Hastings is a lovely woman. She's
not a child. She has a maturity and a faith about her
that tell me she's been through some difficult times.
I believe that's how she learned to truly trust in God.
That's probably why she connects so well with the
children at Byways."

"How can you tell that? You barely know her."

Winifred sniffed.

"I've known Olivia longer than you have, son.
She goes to my church, she sings in my choir, she

attends Bible study when I do. I've had many conversations with her and none of them, not one," she reiterated forcefully, "has led me to believe she has anything to hide."

"But…" Reese groped for an explanation. "How can you tell? What do you see that I'm missing?"

"Oh, you see it, boy." Winifred smiled, that sly, cunning upturn of her lips that meant she understood what he refused to admit. "You see exactly how wonderful Olivia Hastings is. But because you're afraid of what you've begun to feel, because you're scared God will snatch away any good thing that comes into your life, you put up roadblocks."

"I'm not putting up anything."

"What is this sudden distrust of her, then? Are you going to take the word of a man you know is trying to undermine her?" Winifred's dislike of Nelson was obvious. "You think Olivia is hiding something? She probably is. We're all keeping some parts of ourselves secret."

"I'm not." Reese swallowed hard when his grandmother sniffed.

"Really?" she murmured. "Have you told Olivia how you hate sitting in church because inside your heart you're so angry you want to rant at God? Have you told her that your anger has festered for so long that now you cling to it like a security blanket?"

"I—"

"I didn't think so." Winifred's voice softened, her hand brushed his shoulder, touched his cheek so tenderly. "Have you ever asked Olivia point-blank about her past?"

"No, but I've asked questions. She always puts me off or gives the least possible information," he said, indignant that he should have to justify.

"Why do you think that is, Reese?"

"Because there's something she doesn't want me to know?" he blurted.

"Could it be that Olivia hears your doubts every time you push her for explanations? And maybe your doubts add to her fear that she can't tell you what's in her heart because you won't understand?" She wrapped an arm around him and hugged him close for a moment. "Darling boy, please, stop stalling. Open your heart and your mind and ask Olivia to tell you the truth, or let it go."

"I can't."

"I know."

"What does that mean?"

"You won't ask because you're afraid of the answers you'll get. You're afraid that maybe Olivia is exactly who your heart thinks she is, that you'll be drawn into a deeper relationship, one where you'll have to let your heart become involved."

"Grandmother." Reese didn't know what to say.

"Admit it, son. Loving Olivia would mean you have to stop standing on the sidelines of life, as you've done ever since you joined this family. That's the sad thing." She stared right at him. "You never do *really* engage as a member of the family, Reese.

I had hopes with Taylor, but when she died—well, you've never let anyone past that rigid self-reliance."

He couldn't offer any defense.

"We wanted to console you, to help you move on, but you've always kept us at arm's length. That's not what families are about, Reese."

"I know that."

"Do you? Families are about being real, letting down your guard." Winifred brushed his cheek with her fingertips. "It's awkward to confide in someone you aren't sure you can trust. Isn't that how you feel about God?"

"Yes," he admitted. "But I wasn't talking about my shortcomings. I was talking about Olivia. Every time I try to figure out how who she was made her who she is, she backs off."

"And you don't understand that?" Winifred smiled when he shook his head. "Olivia lives her faith in God. It permeates every part of her life, every decision she makes. You don't share that faith. You're not on equal footing and that's a barrier only you can do something about."

"You think I should go back to church, that then she'll tell me the truth?" he asked, dubious about that possibility.

"No." Anger spots dotted Winifred's pale cheeks. "You pretending church isn't going to help anyone."

"Then what are you saying?"

"Take a look at your life, Reese. Is it better without God in it? Are you happier?"

He glared at her, but refused to enter her debate.

"God is your adoptive parent. He loved you so much He gave His son a death sentence just so you could join the family. God loves you. You can't earn it, you can't buy it, and you can't deserve it. All you can do is accept it."

"But Taylor… How can I accept that?"

"By accepting that your Father knows best. And as your Father, He is doing the very best for you."

"Daddy?" Brett wandered into the room, rubbing his eyes. "Are we going home now?"

"Yes, son." Reese wordlessly apologized to Winifred. "I better go."

"You're their father. Your family belongs together." She rose and, against his orders, insisted on opening the door for him to set Brett in his car seat. Winifred waited at the car while he fetched Brady.

Reese used the time inside to call his parents.

"I think she needs to see a doctor," he said hurriedly. "She's pretending otherwise, but she's not well."

They promised to come immediately. Reese hung up, then carried Brady outside and secured him in the car.

"Thank you, Grandmother." He held her carefully, a precious, gentle flower that could so easily wither.

"Good night, Reese." She brushed his cheek with her lips. "I love you."

"I love you, too, Grandmother. Very much." He watched her move to the doorway, framed by the forsythia she adored. He waited until he saw his father's car lights turn down the street, then climbed in his car and drove home.

Since the twins were already in their pajamas, it was quick work to put them to bed. But as he was about to leave the room, Brady spoke.

"Daddy?"

"Yes, son."

"Why were you and Great Granny arguing? Are you mad at her? Isn't she going to be our grandmother anymore, like Mommy isn't our Mommy now?" He sounded scared. "Aren't we going to have our family at our birthday party tomorrow?"

"Oh, yes, son. You're going to have all your family here," Reese assured him.

"Good. 'Cause me and Brett don't want to be alone."

"Yeah," Brett said from the other bed. "Who would look after us when you can't, Daddy? We need our family."

"We sure do." He swallowed the lump in his throat and knelt by Brady's bed. "Did you say your prayers tonight?"

"We forgot."

"How about if you say them now while I listen?"

As their sweet voices talked to God about Emily and Olivia and all the kids at preschool, Reese let his tears fall unchecked. He'd made his own sons afraid they'd lose the ones they loved the most, the ones they trusted.

He'd been so angry at God the Father's decisions. But what kind of a father was he?

Chapter Nine

Olivia tapped on the front door again, a little louder this time.

What was the proper protocol when you showed up on a man's doorstep at eight-thirty in the morning and he didn't answer?

"Yeah?" Reese bleary eyes blinked at her. "Olivia? Uh, what—"

"Well, this is embarrassing. I'm guessing you forgot you asked me to help with the boys' birthday party today. I'll come back later." She turned, went down the stairs quickly, eager to escape.

"Uh, no. Hey!" Reese followed, grabbed her arm. "Wait, please. Birthday." He closed his eyes. "Party. Right. Come inside. If you wouldn't mind making coffee while I shower, that would speed clarity."

"You're a con artist," she said, studying him. "Okay, I'll make coffee. Because I think I'm going to need a cup. Are the boys still—never mind, I see one is up. Happy Birthday, Brett. I thought you were staying overnight at Winifred's."

"We didn't," Brett explained trying to see behind her back, obviously looking for a gift. Brady appeared beside him, rubbing his eyes.

"Come on everyone, inside before the neighbors join us." Reese waited till they'd obeyed then closed the door. He glanced at her, an unspoken question in his eyes.

"Coffee. Got it. Go shower," Olivia told him. "We'll start breakfast. Or something," she added, staring at the mess in the kitchen.

"I was going to clean it up, but I haven't—"

"Reese?" Olivia touched his arm. "Go."

Once he'd left the room, she coaxed the boys into helping her load the dishwasher. Reese returned, freshly shaven with damp hair as the coffee finished brewing. The twins sat in the sunshine on the back deck, happily crunching their cereal.

"Wow! You work fast."

"I try. Here's your coffee. Cereal?" He nodded so she poured a bowl and passed the milk. "Maybe you should tell me who is coming to this birthday."

"Tonight's the family. I'm taking the twins and their friends to a pizza place next week."

"Is it to be a dinner or…" Every time he answered she gave another question until she had an idea of what he'd planned.

"I figured we could turn it into a backyard event if the weather was decent. And it looks like it is."

"You've ordered the cake, bought supplies?" Olivia could tell by his expression that Reese had done almost no preparation. "I think we're going to need Emily to help us get ready. Can you call her?"

Reese gave her an odd look as if to ask why she didn't call.

Olivia turned away, busying herself with turning on the dishwasher. No way would she take the chance of talking to Nelson today. Ever since Olivia had overheard him berating Emily a few days ago, Nelson had begun questioning everyone at Byways about her. That behavior had doubled after Nancy's call. She knew he was trying to turn her focus off his horrid treatment of his sister, but his questions scared her.

Olivia would use every means she could to get Emily separated from her brother. If she had to use Reese and the twins' birthday to help, fine. Protecting that young girl was worth the effort. Especially since she didn't yet know what Nelson was capable of doing.

She scribbled a list of items they would need while listening to Reese on the phone.

"We can pick up Emily in half an hour," he said from behind her.

"Great."

It took only a few minutes for the boys to finish their cereal and dress. They stopped at the bakery first. Fortunately, both boys wanted the same stock cake, which only needed their names added. When they pulled up at Emily's house, she was ready and waiting for them with coupons in hand. They grocery shopped and were back home before noon.

"Okay, Em's got them busy on the trampoline. What shall we do first?" Reese asked.

"You could prepare the vegetables for the tray."

"Kitchen duty. Great." He rolled his eyes.

"Or vacuum the living room."

"I love kitchen duty." He began cleaning celery, carrots and cauliflower.

"I'll mix up the dip. We'll need to scrub the potatoes for baking and season the meat. After that, maybe a quick run-through to tidy the house?"

"Excellent. KP and cleaning. What fun."

Olivia laughed at him. But when their eyes met, the laughter died in her throat as a zap of awareness set her nerves on high. She busied herself with the dip and gradually the tension eased, allowing them to work together. Occasionally, Reese would ask her a question, but mostly he seemed comfortable with the silence between them.

Olivia debated ways of bringing up Emily's situation so she could ask Reese's help. But a birthday party wasn't the place to discuss it. She'd have to wait.

"Okay, food's ready. House is almost clean." He called in the boys and Emily. "Now it's time to get your birthday gifts. Are you ready?"

"Ready," the twins squealed, excitement bubbling over into little jigs of joy.

"I should go home. I'll come back later," Olivia murmured, feeling out of place.

"No way. We're all going together. Right guys?"

"Right. C'mon, Olivia." They grabbed her hands, and Emily's, and tugged them both toward the front door. Everyone packed into Reese's car. "Where are we going, Daddy?"

"You'll see." Reese winked at her and Olivia smiled back.

For now, for today, she'd relax and enjoy. Surely God would send the help she needed soon.

Reese's gifts turned out to be new bicycles.

"I noticed you purchased them assembled," Olivia murmured as they drove home. "Very clever."

"Two long Christmas Eves made me a fast learner." He grinned at the boys' explanations about bicycles to Emily. "Do you ride, Emily?"

Emily's face froze. What was that about?

"My bike's, ah, broken. I like to walk anyway," she added quickly. Too quickly.

"Well, if you ever want a bike, I found Taylor's when I was looking for your guitar the other night. I'll trade you a night's babysitting for it, if you want. Otherwise I'm putting it in a garage sale. It's about time I parked my car in that garage."

"You don't want it? You could go for rides with the boys."

"I already have one for that. So what about a trade?"

"It's a deal. Thanks a lot!"

Back at Reese's, Olivia watched Emily shine as she cheered the twins on in a bike race. Throughout the rest of the afternoon and the evening, as the family gathered and everyone got involved in goofy games the twins adored, Emily relaxed more and more until she convulsed in giggles when Reese offered his own version of a knock-knock joke. Away from Nelson, Emily became an ordinary teen, listening avidly as Sara discussed makeup tricks she'd used on a bride.

The only dark spot on the day was Winifred, who arrived late and looked too frail to be there. But no one could persuade her to go home and rest.

"Dad, you're on barbecue detail since Olivia is afraid I'll burn everything."

"I did not say that." She glared at him.

"Didn't have to. Mom, if you could bring out the juice? I think we're all dry. Sara and Cade, you could shuck the corn if you want. Is that everything?" Reese asked. His eyes crinkled at the corners when Olivia pointed to the fridge. "I'm carrying my creation out myself."

"Your creation? I think I contributed." Olivia enjoyed this teasing, fun side of him.

"A little bit of dip, that was your contribution. Practically store made. Big deal. It's the way the vegetables are presented that makes the dip taste good." Reese set the platter in the middle of the table with a grand flourish.

"What happened to the carrots?" his sister Katie asked, trying to keep a straight face. "It looks like someone beat them up."

"Look at the cauliflower. Did you put it through the food processor, Reese?" Sara's nose wrinkled. "Now I know why Mom always assigned you to cleanup duty."

"Cleaning wasn't exactly Reese's strong suit," Fiona murmured. "But this house looks great today, son."

"Thank you." Reese preened.

Sara and Katie exchanged looks then turned their focus on her.

"Olivia?" they singsonged.

"This is a family argument," Olivia protested holding up one hand. "Don't drag me in."

But they did. Into the laughter, into the joy and into their close-knit circle. How could Reese imagine he wasn't a necessary part of this? As he moved around them, snapping pictures left and right, Reese seemed eminently suited to his big, loving family. He looked at his sons exactly the way his father looked at him, with loving, tender glances that brimmed with pride.

This was a man she could fall in love with.

As the world went on turning around about her, Olivia let the knowledge seep from her heart into her brain. She'd loved Trevor with her whole heart. But he was gone. Their love was over.

And Reese was here now. She prized his determined, single-minded devotion to his kids. She appreciated the way he treated his grandmother, with respect and dignity and a touch of teasing that made Winifred blush and smile. She respected the thread of silver at his temples because she knew it was a badge of surviving hard times.

But Reese didn't care for her. He didn't even trust her. And maybe he never would if Nelson exposed her past. Anyway, Reese thought he had to earn love, do something that would prove he was worthy.

Olivia knew a relationship between them was impossible. She wouldn't risk what her past might do to his family, his future. Maybe not today or tomorrow, but soon a reporter would appear and anyone around her could be caught in the publicity. That's why she'd insisted Nelson handle the media aspect of Byways's new programs and leave her out of it. In retrospect, Olivia now realized that might have been a mistake. Ever since the break-in, he'd been a little too chummy with a local reporter.

Yet Olivia ached for Reese's acceptance. And how could she gain acceptance when she kept parts of her life hidden? Reese might have problems accepting love, but Olivia had her own difficulties worrying that the past might affect her future.

"Is everything all right, dear?" Fiona's beautiful face wore a frown.

"Everything's fine. Wonderful. It's—um, been a while I've been to a child's birthday party. They're such special times, aren't they? Milestones that a parent never forgets, though the child may."

"Yes. A parent's job is a gift and labor."

Fiona studied her with an intensity that made Olivia uncomfortable. The woman was extremely astute. In a minute she'd be asking questions and Olivia did not want the focus on her.

"I think it's cake time," she whispered to Reese who seemed content to sit and watch his twins.

"Yes, of course. Will you help me, Olivia?" He waited beside her, his face very close.

"Sure." She rose, smiled self-consciously at his family and followed him inside.

Reese seemed in no hurry to place the candles on the cakes or to light them. Instead he spent several moments studying her.

"Thank you," he said finally.

"For what? I didn't do anything."

"Yes, you did. You've done a great deal." Reese brushed some invisible crumbs off the counter. He took his time pretending to throw them away before he met her gaze. "Ever since Taylor died, family visits always consisted of them taking charge. Today, for the first time, the family really is my guest."

"I'm not sure that's how they want to feel." She chuckled at his frown. "Your family doesn't expect to be waited on, Reese. They understand, and I think they even enjoy helping you." She debated the wisdom of saying anything more now, but when would be better? "Why do you always call them 'the' family? They're *your* family, Reese. Surely you can't deny that?"

He handed her a packet of candles. Olivia placed five on each cake.

"It's not that I want to deny it," he mumbled. "It's

more that I guess I haven't been able to accept it. I know the problem is me, not them. I intend to work on that."

"Good. So you'll let them help with the Chicago situation?" she whispered, hope lighting inside her as he lit the candles.

"Not yet." He glanced at her, his chin jutting out in determination. "But I'll think about it. Are you ready?"

She nodded, lifted Brett's cake and followed Reese outside, singing "Happy Birthday." The rest of his family quickly joined in, including the twins' high-pitched squeals. Their eyes bugged with excitement. Olivia picked up Reese's camera and began snapping as he helped each son think of a wish. She snapped a picture as they blew out their candles and prayed a silent prayer for them. Around the table she went, adding memory upon memory of the twins' amazing family. They were so lucky to have loved ones.

Without warning, a small, heart-shaped face swam into Olivia's vision. The pain stabbed its familiar jab through her heart and she froze.

Help me, Father.

"Olivia?"

It seemed Reese's voice came from far away, though he stood in front of her, holding out a plate with cake and ice cream on it. But somehow she couldn't break free of the past. Not until everyone turned to stare at her and it was too late to pretend nothing was wrong.

"Excuse me." She handed him his camera. "I'll get some more juice." She fled into the house before anyone could stop her and hid out in the bathroom, praying for strength and courage. Finally the need to weep had passed and she was back in control.

"Are you all right, Olivia?" Winifred sat in the kitchen, her astute gaze assessing. "Is something wrong?"

"No. Just memories." Precious memories. She pasted on a smile. "I'm fine."

"Then come join us. It's time for the twins to open their gifts."

No one asked any probing questions or stared at her, but Olivia knew they were curious. Reese, most of all. She flashed him a cheery smile and produced the boys' presents, promising she'd help them fly the box kites as soon as they put them together.

The afternoon drained into evening. When Winifred drooped, her son insisted on taking her home. When Thomas returned, his face was troubled. The two small boys also grew wearier with each passing hour. The Woodwards were perceptive people. It wasn't long before Fiona whisked her husband away, claiming leftover work at Weddings by Woodwards as her excuse. Cade and Sara promised the boys a ride on the ponies and Katie assured them they'd have time for one more trip to their favorite water park before summer's end. Katie offered to drop Emily off at her home. She and Reese packed Emily's bike into the back of her SUV.

"Thank you very much." Emily grinned. "I'll babysit whenever you want."

"I'll hold you to that, Em." Reese hugged her. "Thanks for coming today." He slipped some money into her pocket and when she tried to object, hushed her. "You really helped us out. I appreciate it." He ruffled her hair fondly.

"Hey, you two munchkins, I need one more hug." Katie gathered the twins in her arms and began tickling them.

Since Reese was answering the phone, Olivia grabbed the opportunity to talk to Emily alone. She led her outside the front door.

"Have you thought any more about what I said?"

"Yes." Emily bit her bottom lip, her face bleached of all color. "I'm fine, Olivia, but I can't say anything. Please don't ask me anymore."

"I won't, honey. All I want is for you to promise that if ever you need someone, if you need to talk or get away or anything, you'll call me. I got this for you." She slid the small cell phone into Emily's hand.

"I can't take that. I can't pay you," Emily whispered, glancing over her shoulder as if afraid someone watched them.

"I don't want pay. I'm lending it to you. The ringer is turned off so no one will hear." Like Nelson. "My numbers are programmed in just in case you ever need to call. Ever. Okay?" She waited, hoping the girl would agree.

Experience told Olivia that sooner or later Emily

was going to need someone. And she intended to be that person.

"But what if—"

"Anytime. I'll do whatever I need to do to keep you safe, Emily. You can trust me," she added as Katie came out the door. "You only have to ask for help."

"Thanks." Emily slid the phone into her pocket then climbed into Katie's vehicle.

Reese and the boys stood outside and they all waved as the group drove away.

"Daddy?" Brett tugged on his father's pant leg. "Can you carry me?"

"Sure I can." Reese swung the boy up to his shoulder. "Tired, huh?"

"Birthday's are hard work," Brady agreed as he grabbed Reese's free hand. "Can you swing me?"

Reese glanced at her as if asking for help. Olivia held out one hand, he held out another and together they swung Brady into the house.

"Bath time, guys." Reese shooed them into their room to remove their clothes. "You," he said to Olivia, steering her toward the family room, "sit down and relax. You've done enough today."

"I should go home." And avoid bedtime.

"Not yet. Please?"

"I'll stay a little longer."

"Thanks." Reese smiled and left. A moment later the bathroom door closed and water began gushing into a tub.

Olivia went to clear up the kitchen, but there wasn't much left to do. Katie and Fiona must have loaded the dishwasher. Everything had been carried inside, leaving the patio immaculate. But there were bits of food to put away, the leftover cakes to cover and the counters to wipe down. When that was finished, Olivia put the kettle on for tea then returned to the family room.

She'd only meant to rest her eyes, but two giggling children told her she'd fallen asleep. She growled like a grumpy bear and snapped her teeth.

"Olivia is a tiger," Brett said.

"She looks like a kitten," Reese murmured. He smiled at her. "Want to share our bedtime story, Olivia?"

"Of course."

"It's about a king," Brady whispered as he climbed into her lap. He settled himself comfortably against her chest, hand tucked against his cheek. "Ready, Daddy."

Brett had taken up the exact same position on Reese's lap. "I'm ready, too."

Olivia looked at Reese, shared his smile.

"Once upon a time…"

Ten minutes later they tucked both sleeping boys into bed. Reese switched on the night-light then ushered her from the room.

"I don't think there will be any bad dreams tonight," he said. "I suppose you made tea?"

"Black currant."

"I didn't even know I had black currant tea," he said, eyes wide as he accepted the cup she poured and sipped. "Not bad."

"You bought some today." Olivia giggled at his surprise. "It's great for winding down after a long day and it has no caffeine."

"No good for the morning, then." He winked and Olivia laughed, recalling his bleary-eyed stare of earlier today.

"It's a gorgeous evening. Let's sit outside."

The night stilled. Not a breath of air played with the shrubbery around the yard. The heady scent of the flowers filled the air.

"I can hardly believe summer is almost over." Reese's quiet voice reflected the peace of the moment. "It goes so quickly. The boys will start school soon."

"That will be a big change for all of you." Olivia didn't want to harp, but wasn't it time Reese admitted the truth to his family? "What will you do about Chicago?"

"I got an idea this afternoon. Grandmother said something that made me think of a new angle. I'll try it on Mrs. Garver next week. And you?"

She blinked, started by the comment.

"What do you mean 'me'?"

"Olivia, it's very obvious that there is something about your past that you're not telling everyone. I hope you know you can trust me."

She chose to remain silent, unwilling to confirm or deny his statement.

"I've asked you about your past repeatedly in the last weeks. It's not that I think you've done anything wrong," he rushed to assure her. "But something is off. There are gaps in time that you don't explain."

"Don't I have the right to keep some things private? I don't know every detail about your past."

"No," Reese admitted. "But you could. I'm not trying to hide anything."

"Really?" She turned to face him. "Then why don't you tell your family about Chicago?"

"I want to find a resolution before I bother them with it."

"Baloney. I'm a child psychologist, Reese. But I can understand adults, too."

"What does that mean?"

"It means I think you're hiding behind your past. Somewhere inside you is a little four-year-old boy who was left in a store. You're afraid, consciously or subconsciously, that the Woodwards will dump you when they know about Chicago."

To her surprise he mused on that for a moment before nodding.

"You could be right. I think we're all products of our pasts." His dark eyes held hers. "But at least I've admitted mine and I'm trying to deal with it."

"No, you're not," Olivia snapped, irritated that he still refused to acknowledge the truth. "You're trying to make sure it doesn't happen again."

"I don't want to let Grandmother down—"

"Who says you'd let her down?" She smiled sadly

at the stubborn thrust of his chin. "You don't trust your own family to understand your problem, Reese. How can I trust you to understand mine?"

He stared at her without speaking, and Olivia knew it was time to leave, now, before the intimacy of the night and the ache in her heart combined to release memories she didn't want to remember, memories that would make her more vulnerable to his charm.

"It's time for me to go home." She hurried inside, put her cup in the dishwasher, grabbed her coat and made a beeline for the front door. Reese's hand on her arm stopped her before she could escape.

"Thank you for helping, Olivia. And for the kites. We appreciate you." His voice came low, intimate, his breath moving a tendril of her hair against her ear.

She had to turn and look at him.

"You're welcome," she murmured, studying his beloved face. "Have some trust, Reese. In God, in your family, in yourself." Her head told her to leave, but her heart made her linger, aching for something she couldn't have.

"Olivia—" His hand tightened. "I—"

"Good night," she whispered, then fled.

Reese stood in the doorway long after Olivia's car disappeared. But her words wouldn't leave his brain.

Have some trust in God.

That's what he was afraid of. Trusting and being let down again.

Reese doubted Taylor would say she'd been let

down. She'd died, yes, but she was with her Savior. He couldn't wish her back because that's not what Taylor, with her strong faith in God's love, would have wanted.

Had God really let him down?

For the first time Reese examined his situation in detail. He was healthy, strong, with a great job. He had a family who was there the minute he called, and mostly long before he had to ask. He had no doubts they loved him. Any fool could see their genuine affection. They'd never refused to help him; it had been he who rejected them, refused to be drawn into their circle because he was insecure.

The truth was, Reese needed the Woodwards. They were his children's future if anything happened to him. There was no family on earth he'd trust more to take his place and ensure that his twins were loved.

Lastly Reese considered his two precious sons. Of course they were work. But the family, *his* family, had taught him that every worthwhile thing was work. He would lay his life down for them if he had to.

"So what am I afraid of, God?"

He sat in the darkened peace of his backyard, sipping black currant tea and struggling to puzzle it out. And then, like a star after dusk, an answer lit the chaotic fear smothering his mind.

Vulnerability.

Reese didn't understand that. So he prayed for

further illumination. Instantly he was four again, hiding under the clothes' rack at Weddings by Woodward.

Goodbye, son.

He'd wanted to cry out, to beg her to stay. But she left too quickly and he'd been too afraid to call out. If he had, would she have come back?

That's what lay at the root of his fear—that if he'd asked his mother to take him, if he'd run after her, begged her, she would have left him anyway.

Why did he think that?

Reese probed his memory, but found only fragments of the past, nothing that would tell him more than he already knew. His mother had loved him but she hadn't been able to care for him.

The Woodwards had. He'd never been abused, never felt unloved or longed for someone else's family. Like Olivia, he'd had an ideal childhood. He'd always been their eldest son, their pride and joy. Neither Donovan nor Katie nor Sara had ever made him feel less a Woodward. Winifred hadn't batted an eyelash when, at fourteen, he'd told her he wanted to be a company lawyer, to make things right.

"It's a noble plan, Reese. But remember, God is the only one who can right the wrongs of this world. Sometimes you have to leave it up to Him."

That's what he had to do now. Let go of his fears, his obsession with being worthy, and his determination to repay his family for loving him. The simple truth was he could never repay them, he could only pass it on by teaching his children that love embraced. It never excluded.

It was time to *be* a Woodward.

"Help me, God."

Reese walked inside the house, picked up the phone.

"You know that report I asked for, about Olivia Hastings?"

"I haven't quite finished."

"Shelve it. I don't need to know."

Then Reese dialed Winifred's number. He reached her answering machine, so he called Katie.

"Katie? What's going on?" His heart sank as his sister told him Winifred had been rushed to hospital.

"Pray, Reese. Pray really hard."

He sat in the dark asking God to be with the small, frail woman who'd taught him so much. Tomorrow he'd call a meeting. Together, the Woodward family would decide their next step in Chicago.

But as he sat alone, Reese knew he had just one more thing to do. He had to tell Olivia that he would understand whatever she wanted to tell him. Because Reese needed to hear everything.

Olivia was too precious to let go.

Chapter Ten

The last week of August arrived at Byways with stifling heat, Nelson's complaints and more meetings than Olivia thought possible.

"I feel like the proverbial headless chicken," she told Casey as Wednesday morning's last client left.

"How is the new house?"

"Fantastic. I can't believe I didn't move ages ago. You'll have to come over when I get things in place. I'll cook something on my new barbecue." She laughed as Casey licked her lips. "Don't get excited. I'm not that great a cook."

"You have to be better than me. I burn water." Casey grinned.

"Yes, I'm better than that." She frowned. "I haven't seen Emily around. Have you?'

"Uh, yesterday Nelson said something about her being sick. Maybe she's still feeling rough. You could ask him. 'Scuse me." Casey grabbed the ringing phone.

"I have a better idea." Olivia closeted herself inside her office and dialed the cell phone she'd given Emily.

She'd almost given up hope when she heard a whispered, "Hello."

"Emily, this is Olivia. Are you all right?"

"Y-yes. I'm okay."

She didn't sound okay, she sounded stuffy, as if she'd been weeping.

"Have you been sick?'

"Uh, yeah. But I'm feeling better now."

"Good. Will you be here this afternoon?"

"No!" Her panic was unmistakable.

A hard rap on the door startled Olivia. If it was Nelson she'd ask him to come back.

"Hang on a second, Emily. Someone is at my door."

"Can't. Gotta go." The connection abruptly ended.

Olivia stared at her phone before another thump at the door brought her back to reality.

"Nelson, you really need to learn patience—" She stopped midsentence. Reese stood behind the twins, who were each holding a little bouquet of daisies. "Hello."

"Daddy said I knocked too hard. Did I? I'm strong." Brett shoved the flowers at her. "Thank you for helping with our birthday party."

"Me, too," Brady squealed.

"Thank you. They're lovely."

"They smell nice. You do, too," Brady told her with a grin.

"Thank you." She almost burst out laughing at Brett's curious sniff.

"Here are your cars, guys. You sit down on the mat and play with them while I talk to Olivia, okay?"

Reese waited until they sat before he smiled at her. "You do smell good. And you look good, too."

"Music to my ears. Thank you." Olivia curtsied then frowned at him. "Shouldn't you be at work? And the twins at preschool? Or day care?"

"Slave driver." He chuckled at her raised eyebrow. "Actually, we've come bearing gifts. Of lunch. Don't worry, I didn't make it."

"A picnic?" Olivia saw Nelson watching them from the hallway, a scowl on his face. She'd never get a better opportunity to talk to Reese about Emily, but it had to be somewhere other than Byways. "Wonderful. Where?"

"We have that planned, don't we, guys?"

The twins nodded, chubby cheeks glowing with excitement.

"Can you come to our picnic, Olivia?" Brady asked, pocketing his car.

"I would love to. Just let me get my purse."

They moved into the hall and she locked her door. Nelson had disappeared. But Olivia knew he was watching from somewhere, just as she now knew he'd arranged for someone to break into her office. Three board members had called to tell her someone had contacted them. Nancy had stalled a Denver

reporter who had been given her phone number.
Nelson was digging hard into the past.

"Lead on, gentlemen."

Reese drove them to Cheesman Park.

"I've wanted to come here since the day I arrived,
but tourism's taken a backseat due to work and
house-hunting. It's lovely."

They found a place near the children's playground.
Reese spread a thick quilt on the grass and invited
her to sit. The boys raced over to the slides.

"That should burn some energy," he said. Then he
turned his attention to her. "I haven't seen you in a
while. How are you?"

"I'm fine. Busy. I moved into my house."

"I wish I'd had time to help."

"I heard about Winifred. How is she?"

"Preparing for open heart surgery. We're all on
hold, praying she'll be okay." He smiled. "Thanks for
sending flowers."

"She's a great woman."

"Yes, she is." Reese leaned back, studied her. "Tell
me about your house."

Olivia told him, saw his eyes flare with surprise.

"That's a—nice neighborhood."

"I think so. The house is miles too big for one
person, of course, but it's so long since I've felt
settled that I'm enjoying every bit of space. It has a
pool," she added. "When I get organized, I'll have
you and the boys over for a swim. Though, I guess
with September around the corner, I'll have to hurry."

"Cooler days are coming," he agreed. "But we generally get decent weather in September. We'd love to come. But I need to ask you something else."

"Oh?" She waited, tense.

"The family, my family," he corrected with a grin, "usually spends Labor Day weekend at Gran's cottage. She insists we keep the tradition going even though she can't be there this year. I was hoping you'd be our guest this coming weekend."

"I'd love it," Olivia said impulsively. Then his words penetrated. "*Your* family?"

Reese nodded.

"I took your advice and did some hard thinking," he said. "I've let the past control me too much. I have a great family and it's time I started enjoying them and stopped trying to pay them back."

"What changed your mind?"

"You," he said quietly. "I realized that my attitude hurt them. They felt like I was trying to buy into the family and all they wanted to do was love me."

"Thank God," she murmured.

"I did. Many times." He grinned. "I'm working on that relationship, too."

"I'm glad." Olivia hesitated, but she had to ask. "And Chicago?"

"That's a little tougher assignment." Reese held up a hand when she would have interrupted. "It's not that I'm trying to keep that secret anymore, but with Gran—" He shrugged. "I'm looking at things differently now."

"Good." Olivia studied him. "You can give God a chance to work things out."

"Yeah." Reese's smug smile told her he wasn't totally comfortable with absconding all responsibility. "There's been a new development. A man showed up yesterday at the hospital."

"Really? Who is he?" She waved at the twins, nodded that she had seen them hurtle from the top of the little slide to the bottom. Then she looked at Reese. "Well?"

"My grandfather's stepbrother, Arthur. Grandmother had never met him before. Apparently my grandfather never knew about him. Anyway he introduced himself to her and they're becoming fast friends."

"That's nice."

"Yeah." Reese waved the twins over and began unpacking the picnic basket. Olivia helped serve the children, accepted some salad, a roll and a piece of fried chicken and began eating as Reese, with frequent interruptions from the kids, continued the story.

"At first Art just wanted to know about his stepbrother, whatever Gran could tell him. Now it seems like he's sort of moved into the family."

"Does that bother you?"

Reese made a face, nodded.

"Kind of. I mean, he just waltzes in and bam! He's a Woodward." His face twisted in a funny look. "Stupid, isn't it? That's exactly what I did. I have no right to say that no one else is allowed."

"But the oldest son in you wants to protect the family. It's understandable, Reese." Olivia touched his shoulder then quickly moved her hand. "But if Winifred is happy—"

"She's ecstatic." Reese set down his own plate, his face troubled. "I don't know when I've seen her so radiant."

"But that's a good thing. Isn't it?"

"Yes, of course. It keeps her mind off Chicago, for one thing." He poured the boys a drink. "We've been given the option of buying the Garver property until mid-September. Then it goes on the open market. Developers will snap it up. I want her to get that dream, but—"

"Maybe it's not so important now?" Olivia suggested.

"It's just that I wanted her to have her dream. I wanted to be able to give it to her."

"Nothing wrong with that."

"No." He frowned.

"What aren't you saying?"

"Olivia, I don't want to worry her. I want Winifred comfortable, healthy, carefree. But I've got to think of the business."

"And?" She dabbed at Brady's lips, wiped his hands and poured more juice.

"Weddings by Woodwards doesn't go into hiatus when someone is ill. It's basically a service business that depends on word of mouth and our reputation is our trading card. We can't go on hold while the head of the company recuperates. It sounds horrible to say, but if we're not doing Chicago, that decision has to be made so I can use our option clause with the renovators, the fittings suppliers and the stock people." He pushed his plate away, frustration evident. "My job is to protect the company, Olivia."

"You're saying someone needs to make a decision."

"Soon. Yes. We have a plan for her getting ill, but it never included deciding on Chicago." He wiped down Brett and agreed the boys could go and play for a little while longer. "But only a few minutes. I have to get back to work and you have preschool."

The twins scampered away, energy restored.

"You're a psychologist, Olivia. How do I get my family to understand that we have to start looking at options?"

"You say exactly that. You don't have to scare them. They're already worried about her and probably feeling helpless. Maybe the best thing is to give each of them a job, something they can do that looks into other options you could take." She touched his hand, drawing his attention. "You said it's not urgent?"

"Not yet."

"Then make them understand that. This weekend, when you're all together, might be the perfect time to get the issue on the table. They know about the offer to purchase?" She waited for his nod. "Then pose a question about what if the deal falls through?

What's the next step? All you really want them to do is talk about it anyway."

"Particularly Dad. He's so stressed."

"Okay, so the more they bat around ideas, the easier it may be to make a decision if and when that becomes necessary." Olivia smiled, touched his cheek. "She's eighty, Reese. But she's feisty and determined, and she's gone through life fighting."

"You're saying I should clear everything with them, but make the hard decision myself." He swallowed hard, staring at their entwined hands. "Why do I have to be the one to kill her dream? She's always been so good to me, pushed me when I weakened, bolstered me when I would have quit. After Taylor—she was there morning, noon and night." Reese sighed. "I love her. I don't know if I can do it, Olivia."

"Who better, Reese? Katie?"

"She's too occupied with keeping things going. And Sara's not familiar enough with the business yet. Mom and Dad are too close. Winifred is all they can think of."

"You said you have a couple of weeks. Use it. Get the rest of the family unified in at least talking about the future. Together you'll think of something. I know it."

"You have a lot of faith in me." Reese grasped her other hand and pulled her to her feet. "Why is that, Olivia?"

She kept her hands in his, met his scrutiny with her own. And felt that reassuring bump of knowledge.

Reese was buried deep in her heart. Trevor still held his place, but her heart had expanded and filled with Reese.

"Because I know who you are, Reese Woodward. I know how determined you are to protect your family, how much you love them."

"Yes, I do," he acknowledged freely. "I thank God for them, for the love they've showered on me, though I've done nothing to deserve it."

Olivia smiled, withdrew one hand and pointed at the twins.

"Could they do anything to make you love them more than you do now?" she asked him quietly.

He glanced at the boys, but his eyes returned to hers. "No."

"That's the way it is with God. He already loves us so much. All we can do is love Him back."

"I'm beginning to understand that." His watch beeped. He squeezed her fingers and released them before whistling at the boys. "Come on. I've got a meeting to prepare for. Let's pack up."

Amid the twins' grumbling, Olivia helped Reese stuff everything back into the picnic basket. As they walked across the grass he began to laugh.

"What's so funny?"

"Every time I see you, it seems like I'm dumping my worries on you. And you never refuse to listen. You kindly help me up then point me in the right direction with encouragement and hope. You're a very special woman, Olivia."

"I didn't do anything," she protested, feeling both proud and shy. "Only listened." She watched fondly as the twins raced ahead playing tag.

"Now it's my turn. What's been happening with you?"

Here was the opportunity she needed.

"I overheard Nelson bawling out Emily a while ago." She pursed her lips. "It was not pleasant. I found Emily weeping later, though she pretended she had something in her eye. Nelson has realized that I'd overheard."

"So now maybe he'll get a grip." Reese checked her face, frowned. "He won't?"

"I think his abusive language toward her has escalated."

"Because?" Reese's face grew tight, anger darkening his eyes.

"Because she hasn't been at Byways for two days. She loves it there, you know that."

He nodded, his face thoughtful.

"I gave her a cell phone after the twins' party so she could call me if she needed help. She didn't call, but today I called her." Olivia inhaled to control her fear. "Reese, she sounded horrible. I don't know what to do. I'm afraid for her, afraid of what he might do."

"Why did Nelson say Emily wasn't at Byways?"

"He told Casey she was sick yesterday. That was not illness I heard in her voice, it was fear. I've tried and tried to get her to talk to me. But she won't admit it. She won't say anything against her brother."

They reached the car. Reese buckled in one twin while Olivia did the other. He held open her door, but when she came around to the side of the car, he stopped her from entering.

"You want to see her, to assess the situation, don't you?"

"I'd like to, but I'm not sure how to go about it."

"What if we stopped by with an ice cream treat? I could say I was wondering how the bike was working out. Or the twins could invite her for a bike race or something. Or maybe, we heard she was sick and wanted to cheer her—"

"You genius!" Olivia stood on her tiptoes, leaned forward and kissed him on the lips before her brain reminded her that was not the appropriate response for a friend. "Oh." She felt her face burn. "Sorry."

"Why are you sorry?" His dark eyes glowed as he leaned against the car. His arms slid around her waist, drawing her nearer. "I'm not complaining. In fact—" he tilted his head and kissed her. "I'm quite enjoying this," he murmured into her hair when she turned her head.

"Reese."

"Yes?"

"We're in public. The twins are watching."

"Uh-huh." His fingers grazed the nape of her neck, nuzzled the skin just beneath her earlobe. "And?"

"I'm embarrassed." She shifted, reviving all the reasons this couldn't happen. "I'd been trying and trying to think of an excuse to go over there, to see her, you know?"

"I know." Reese held her close, his chest rumbling under her cheek. "To see if there are any marks, any signs of abuse. Mother Olivia and that tender heart."

Something in the way he said that made her tip back to study his face.

"I'm not a bleeding heart," she said. "But Emily is like family and—"

"You can't help yourself from helping." He bussed her chin with his fist. "I know."

"Daddy?"

"Yes, Brett?" Reese didn't move a muscle. "What is it?"

"Will I get in trouble if I tell Great Granny she was right?"

"Right about what, son?" Reese pushed a tendril of hair off her forehead then traced her eyebrow.

"Great Granny told Grandma you an' Olivia would soon be kissing. Can I tell her she was right?"

Olivia eased out of his arms and turned her head to hide her laughter. And to cover her embarrassment. Reese's family had been discussing her? Kissing him?

"I think we should keep it a secret," Reese answered his son as he waited for Olivia to climb inside. He winked as he closed the car door. "After all, this family should have some secrets, don't you think?"

"I like secrets." Brett clapped his hands.

"Me, too," Brady said. "How far is the ice cream store?"

Reese rounded the car and slid into the driver's seat.

"Proof that little pitchers have big ears," Reese growled as he shifted into gear. "One ice cream store coming up."

They bought a cake with a cat on it and drove to Emily's.

Knocking at the front door did not produce Emily, but Brett's bellow did. She opened the door warily.

"Hi."

"Hi, Em. We heard you weren't feeling well so we brought you an ice cream cake. It seems to cheer the twins up all the time."

"Um." Emily glanced at Olivia.

"We needed Olivia to come along to hold the cake. We're celebrating."

"Celebrating what?" Emily looked from one to the other.

"Olivia bought a new house. It has a swimming pool."

"Really?" Emily winced when the boys yanked on her arm. Reese reined them in.

"As soon as I get things shipshape you're coming over. Aren't you?"

"For a housewarming," Reese added. "Can we come inside? The cake is melting."

"I guess." Emily looked past them before finally opening the door.

"How are you feeling?"

"I'm all right, Olivia. You didn't have to worry about me."

"I always worry about you, sweetie. I care about what happens to you." Olivia caught her worried look when the twins bumped a plant stand. "Let's get this cake cut. That will keep the kids busy," she whispered.

"Okay."

As Emily gathered plates, a knife, cutlery, Olivia watched her. The cabinets were arranged in scrupulous precision. Even the paper napkins were perfectly aligned.

"You keep the house so neat," she praised. "I wish my place looked like this."

Emily said nothing, but her cheeks paled.

"On the phone you said you're feeling better. What was it, a stomach bug?"

"Uh, yeah. I guess." Emily would not look at her.

"Do you need anything?" Reese asked. "Some ginger ale or something?"

"No, thanks. I'm fine. Oh, dear."

Brett dropped a blob of ice cream on the floor. Emily jumped up, wetted a paper towel and scrubbed at the linoleum with a fierceness that shocked Olivia. She glanced at Reese pointedly.

"My hands are so sticky." Olivia smiled. "Emily, may I use the bathroom?"

Emily jumped up, clearly wanting to say no. Finally she nodded.

"Through there."

"Thank you."

The room was small, but extremely tidy. The mirror glistened. The sink shone. The floor could have been china, it was so white. The towels were perfectly aligned on the rack. Olivia dried her hands then did her best to return them to their former precision. Was there another teenage girl in the Western world who had a bathroom this spotless?

"Thanks, Emily." Olivia pretended surprise at the time on the kitchen clock. "Reese, I have to go. I've a hundred things to do this afternoon."

He took her cue and used paper towels to clean up the kids and wipe off the table.

"Sorry we didn't call first, Em. I didn't even think of it. I hope we didn't disturb you. I know when you don't feel well, company isn't always fun."

"I keep telling you I'm fine," Emily shot back somewhat desperately.

"Good. You keep the rest of the cake for dessert tonight," he said.

"I'll see you tomorrow?" Olivia hugged her, felt the girl catch her breath. "Did I hurt you?"

"No. I'm fine." Emily moved to the door, held it open. Only for the twins did her old smile reappear. "See you, guys."

"Can you race us on our bikes sometime? That's why we came here." Brett looked at his dad. "Was that a secret?"

"Nope. That's what you wanted to ask, I think."

Reese grinned at Emily. "They think they're pros on wheels now."

"I haven't had a chance to practice, but when I do, you better be ready." She tickled Brady.

"C'mon guys. Way past time for preschool."

Soon they were all in the car. Emily stayed near the door, but she did wave at them. Right after she checked to see if anyone was watching. As they drove away, Reese switched on a children's tape. When the boys were happily singing along, he turned to Olivia.

"You're worried about her, aren't you?"

"Yes." Olivia pursed her lips. "Did you notice the way she cringed when I hugged her? She's hurting and I'm wondering if—"

"Nelson's the reason," he finished. "I know nothing about abusers, but I have never seen a house as immaculate as that one and Grandmother is a pretty fussy housekeeper."

"The shelves, the towels, the dishes—everything was in exactly the right place."

"Meaning?" His dark eyes met her and she glimpsed sympathy there.

"Meaning many abusers try to exert control by forcing rigid patterns on others. Things placed at certain exact distances. An immaculate house. Have you ever noticed how fastidious Nelson is? There's never even a paper clip out of place on his desk."

"Up to now, I've always admired it." Reese frowned at her. "We still don't have any proof, however. So I want you to stay out of his path."

"Don't think I haven't been. I've been so scared he'd take something out on Emily, I go out of my way to avoid him." Olivia bit her lips. "She can't stay there, Reese. I've been praying and praying for a way to help her and nothing's clear except that I know she can't stay there."

"I know." His hand covered hers. His smile warmed her. "We'll have to pray together. If there's one thing I learned from you, Olivia, it's that God answers. He always answers."

"And Emily is His child. Thanks for reminding me." She opened her door as soon as he pulled into the parking lot at Byways. "See you, boys."

"See you, Olivia." After a two-second interval they returned to their singing.

"Olivia?" Reese got out of the car, came up beside her. "About this weekend and the lake?"

"Oh, yes. I'd almost forgotten." She smiled at him. "I'd love to come. I'll even help you broach the subject of Chicago if you haven't yet."

He shook his head though his grin was wide. "I tried, but I haven't been able to get everyone together yet."

"Then this weekend." She stopped when he shook his head.

"You'd get me into trouble for sure. Grandmother has a no-work policy at the beach. It's the first time in years that the family doesn't have a big event for the Labor Day weekend so I think everyone's looking forward to a little R & R."

"Shall I drive up?"

"I'll pick you up on Friday. Here or at your place. Whichever."

"Here," she decided. "We've got the end of summer festival all day. I could be late."

Reese didn't seem perturbed. He leaned forward, touched her chin with one finger.

"It will be my pleasure to wait for you, Olivia." He grinned when she backed up. "No kissing?"

"Definitely no kissing," she warned. "Nelson is watching."

"I'm getting tired of Nelson," he complained. "At least he can't come to the beach."

"Can Emily?" She shouldn't have asked. "I know it's rude," she apologized. "But the very idea of Emily, alone with him when I'm not around, worries me."

"Of course she'll come. I'll get Grandmother to call Nelson. No one can refuse my grandmother."

"You would use your poor sick grandmother? And here I am thinking you're such a paragon of fatherhood." Olivia tsk-tsked.

"Oh, I am," he said, his face straight. "But if Emily comes along, she'll get the kids involved in something and you and I will have time to talk. Maybe then you can tell me about your secrets and why you look like you're about to burst into tears whenever my sons hug you."

Too shocked to answer, Olivia stood and watched as he touched his forefinger to his lips and then pressed it against her cheek.

A moment later Reese and the twins disappeared from sight. Behind Olivia, the gravel rattled underfoot. She was no longer alone and Nelson's sneaking around was getting to her.

"Does he know you're not who you claim to be, Olivia?"

Emily's frightened face filled her mind.

"Who are you pretending to be, Nelson?" Olivia demanded before hurrying inside.

Chapter Eleven

"Welcome to Woodward Lodge, Olivia. And you, too, Em."

It was not the most auspicious of beginnings. Rain that had held off for most of Byways's Festival Day had followed them all the way from the city into the mountains. A chilly rain that clung to the towering spruce and pine like a misty bridal veil.

Reese sincerely hoped it would not last the weekend.

"It's beautiful. It looks like it's been here a hundred years." Olivia tilted her head back to study the stone building with its levels and terraces. "It looks welcoming."

"Winifred always insists Dad build a big fire in the hearth room. You and Emily take the boys. I'll bring the luggage." He weighed suitcases. "How come Emily only needs a backpack and you need one suitcase while the boys and I have four?"

"It's a girl thing," Emily teased. She grinned at Olivia.

The boys raced ahead, legs churning to be the first one up. Reese was content to trail behind. After his comment about secrets, he'd half expected Olivia to find a reason to opt out. He should have known better. His lady was nobody's weakling.

"Olivia, my dear. How are you?" Fiona welcomed her as his grandmother would have, with a hug and a cup of tea. Olivia would love that. "And there are my sweet boys. Hello, darlings."

From the sound of Brett and Brady, they were being soundly kissed.

"Does anyone care that I'm loaded with luggage and getting soaked?" he called.

Sara stuck her head out the door. "No." She giggled and let it slam shut.

"Brat," he muttered, brightening when Cade stepped outside and helped him bring in his load. "Thanks, man."

"No problem. But this better cancel out the dunking you threatened Sara with."

Reese shook his head sadly. "She's got you hog-tied," he grumbled.

"And you're jealous. I understand." Cade grinned and went to cuddle with his wife.

"Take your shoes off at the door, Reese. I hate—"

"Stepping in puddles. I know already!" He grinned at Olivia. "You remember Katie? She's a wimp about getting wet unless it's from a diving board fifty feet above a pool. Figure that out. If she hears about your pool, she'll be knocking on your door when we go home."

Olivia seemed delighted that someone wanted to use her diving board. The two women were soon deep in discussion. Having delivered the luggage to the appropriate rooms, Reese changed clothes and went back downstairs in search of food.

"Anyone heard from Donovan lately?" He snitched two of his mother's lemon crunch cookies.

"Your brother was never one for letters, and he hasn't changed." His father slapped his hand away from the potatoes he was mashing. "We'll all eat, together, son."

"Soon?" Reese pleaded.

"Yes, if you'll get out of the kitchen," Fiona grumbled. But she slipped him a couple of carrots. "Try these."

Olivia's laughter drew him to the hearth room. She was curled up in front of the fire playing chutes and ladders with Brett as if she'd been coming here for years. Reese sat down beside her, enjoying the way she seemed to fold in with his family. Cade had Emily and Brady busy at the windows, checking the lake through binoculars.

"Okay?" Reese murmured, leaning closer to Olivia.

"Fine." She smiled and the day lost its gloom.

"Olivia knows how to sail, Reese."

He blinked at Sara, then at Olivia. "Really?"

"I lived on the East Coast for a while. I used to sail quite a lot." She glanced from one to the other of them. "Is that a good thing?"

"Very good." Sara's smile flashed. "He's been bugging Cade and me to go with him. Cade's not really a sailor."

"I'll be glad to go. It must be hard to take the twins by yourself." Olivia's smile wavered. "You look funny. Did I say something wrong?"

"No." He tried to put the pieces together. "How long did you live in the East?"

"A while."

"Where, exactly?"

"What is this—twenty questions?" She pretended to smile, but there was fear crouching in Olivia's eyes.

"Of course not. You don't owe me any explanations." Reese tilted his head toward the game. "I think you've lost."

"I won." Brady giggled. "You have to practice, Olivia."

"Yes, I do." She tickled him until Fiona called them all for dinner.

Reese decided doting grandmothers were a blessing as Fiona took charge of the boys, leaving him free to concentrate on Olivia. If his family would let him.

"Sara said you'd bought a new house," his father said. "Are you enjoying it?"

"It's lovely. I hadn't realized how much I missed having space." She passed him the potatoes, smiled. "The condo was nice enough, but I like to be able to walk outside without taking an elevator."

"She has a swimming pool," Katie explained.

"You're a swimmer?" His father looked faintly surprised.

"I love the water. My grandfather's farm had a pond. I could hardly wait till the ice melted so I could get in it. I won a few medals for diving because Gramps taught me how to hold my breath longer by diving to the bottom of that pond."

It was the most Olivia had ever volunteered about herself. Reese was getting a better picture of her as a child, on a farm, in—Wisconsin, wasn't it?

"It sounds like a happy childhood." His mother promised steamy apple pudding with mugs of hot chocolate for later. "I thought they might take the chill off the evening."

"They will," Olivia said, smiling.

The meal stretched out with the lazy comfort of diners who know there's nothing to rush off to. Sara, Olivia, Emily and Katie insisted on clearing up. Reese used that time to bathe the boys and put them to bed.

"Remember, we're not getting up early and you're not allowed to wake anyone up."

"Not even Grandpa?" Brett scowled. "But he's going to take us fishing early in the morning."

"Really early," Brady confirmed. "Before the

rooster crows." He frowned. "Where do they keep the roosters, Daddy?"

"I'm not sure, son." Reese tucked them in. "But you're not to leave this room or make any noise until Grandpa or I come and get you."

"Can you help us say our prayers, Daddy?" Brett yawned. "Sometimes I forget parts."

"I think God understands what you mean to say," Reese told him, feeling his way on a subject he wasn't sure of. "You do your best. I'll stay and listen."

The twins 'God Bless' list was long and included a number of their friends from preschool, Byways, the neighbors, Emily, the entire family, but especially Olivia.

"And please help Daddy not to kiss Olivia anymore if she doesn't like it," Brett prayed. He paused for a moment as if reconsidering. "But help her to like it 'cause we really like Olivia an' we don't want her to go away. Amen."

"Why would Olivia go away, Brett?"

"I dunno." He snuggled down in his bed until the covers came to his ears. "She came here so she must have gone away from somewhere else. Sometimes I think she wants to go back."

"What makes you think that?"

"'Cause she gets sad."

"Olivia doesn't have a grandpa and grandma and a great granny Win like we do," Brady informed him.

"How do you know?"

"I asked her," he said with great simplicity. "Good night, Daddy."

"Good night." The hugs felt a little sweeter tonight. They were growing so fast. Soon they wouldn't want or need him to listen to their prayers or tuck them in. "Help me be a good father," Reese whispered as he lingered in the doorway.

It felt strange to talk to God again. Strange, yet right. Reese wasn't certain where this new quest to be closer to God would lead, but at least he was trying. And he felt so much better than when he'd been carrying around that chip of bitterness.

Parenthood still overwhelmed him at times. But he was learning to take one step at a time.

"Everything okay?" Olivia peeked into the room, smiled at the sleepers. "They're so adorable."

"Asleep, yes," he agreed with a dry grin. "Okay, they're adorable awake, too. Want to go for a walk?"

"In the rain?" She wrinkled her nose.

"You won't melt. I guarantee it. And there's a lot to see in the woods at night." Reese wasn't sure why he offered. He only knew he wanted time with her. Alone.

"Fortunately, I brought clothes that can withstand rain. I'll meet you at the back door in five minutes. The others are watching a movie."

"Good. They won't notice we're gone." He tweaked her nose, watched her walk to the bedroom Fiona had assigned.

It took only a few minutes to find his old comfortable rubber boots and the jacket he kept for rainy days. His rain hat had a fish lure pinned to the brim. Taylor, he remembered, then realized the pain was almost gone. Only bittersweet memories lingered.

Reese stepped outside and stood under the eaves to wait, watching the rain spatter everything in the forest.

"If I catch a cold…" Olivia warned as she came around the house.

"I'll bring you hot soup, and tea and tons of blankets," he promised. "Come on. I want to show you something."

They walked to the water's edge at the end of the pier. The rain fell steadily, but there was no strong wind to whip the waves into a frenzy.

"Look over there." Reese pointed to an island barely visible through the mist. "That's my island."

"You own an island?" Olivia raised her eyebrows. "Do I call you *sir?*"

"Master will be good enough." He grinned when she scoffed. "On that island I've been Robinson Crusoe, a pirate, a stranded sailor and a being from outer space. I'm only telling you this so you'll know me better, understand who I am."

"Why?" She studied him, hazel eyes dark and un- fathomable, that gorgeous cinnamon hair not quite hidden under her wide-brimmed hat.

"Because I want to know who you are, Olivia. I want to understand what your childhood was like, who your best friend was, what happened to you to give you such a strong faith in God." He tipped back her head and stared into her eyes. "I want to know *you*."

"You already know me," she protested, but it was a halfhearted argument and they both knew it.

"I know stuff about you, but I'm not certain of exactly who you are beneath the skin." He paused, reconsidered his explanation. "Take Emily, for instance."

"Emily?" She blinked, frowned. "Why?"

"Exactly what I would like to know. Why her? What draws you to her? Why Emily?" He shook his head, spraying wet droplets onto his shoulders. "There are a dozen other young girls who are just as troubled, just as needy, but you focus on Emily. Why is that?"

Olivia seemed puzzled by the question. "Why not?"

Frustration sparked inside his brain, but Reese tamped it down.

"See? That's exactly what I mean. I ask a question, you ask another question. Or you change the subject. And we somehow go off topic every single time. You never really tell me who you are, Olivia."

"But you know who I am. I'm a child psychologist. I work at Byways. You hired me, remember?" Olivia's smile appeared for less than thirty seconds before it fell away. She stared at the soggy ground then met his stare. "What is it you're really asking, Reese?"

Defiance sparkled out green jabs from her hazel eyes, but she did not look away.

"I'm not trying to make you angry," he apologized. "I'm not trying to pick on you." Reese chewed his lip, thinking of a way to phrase one of the thousands of questions he had about her. "Talk to me," he pleaded.

Olivia studied him for several minutes, rain dropping on her upturned chin. She didn't seem to notice. Finally she took his hand and tugged.

"Let's walk."

It was enough. For now.

Reese strolled beside her, pausing to study sparkling silver cobwebs when she did. When she moved on, he did the same.

"I had a great childhood. You know that because I told you. I went to college, got my degrees and built a good career. And then some terrible things happened to me. Things I don't want to talk about," she said hurriedly, when he opened his mouth to interrupt. "Ever."

"Okay."

"It's taken me years to move past the pain. Since I came to Denver I've begun to feel whole. I'm ready to pursue my career again, and I don't want anything from the past to tarnish this new world I'm building."

Reese didn't know what to say, how to discern what she wasn't saying, for surely that was as important as what she had said. But one thing he did know. Behind her words, hidden under the pretense that everything was all right now, lay a world of pain that Olivia would not or could not share.

"Have I scared you off?" She stopped, gazed at him with a hint of fear crouched in her eyes. "Would you prefer if I left in the morning? I could make an excuse, a reason why I had to go—"

"You really don't get it, do you?" Reese faced her and cupped his hands against her dewy cheeks. "I wasn't asking because I was curious, or because I had concerns about you, or because I want you to leave. I want to know more about you because I've begun to care for you, Olivia."

"You have?" Her eyes grew huge and shone with disbelief as she stared at him. "But you can't!"

In that moment Reese knew that nothing he could say would answer any of the questions he had. Nor could he ease her fears. The only thing he could do was be here, listen and wait until Olivia was ready.

He bent his head and kissed her with a tenderness that surprised even himself. He tried to infuse the embrace with all the emotions that filled him. When he'd done his best, he drew back, smiled and traced the furrow of lines on her forehead.

"I don't need to know any more, Olivia." He smiled at her blink of surprise. "I've watched you at Byways, with the kids there, with the twins, with Emily. I know who you are deep inside. When you're ready to tell me more, I'll listen. But I won't push because I need you to trust me, too."

She would've protested, but he shushed her with

another quick kiss, grasped her hand and drew her forward.

"Where are we going now?" She bent her head to hide her eyes.

Reese grinned.

"I'm going to show you some of my favorite haunts. Are you up for it?"

"Anytime," she said, her smile widening. "Lead on."

So he showed her the burger joint, the bowling alley, the corner grocery that carried necessities like mosquito repellent, fireworks and sunscreen. They splashed through the puddles to the dock where planes flew in with customers willing to pay top dollar.

"And this," Reese said, leading her through a tangle of underbrush, past giant ferns and beneath massive spruce trees whose boughs dripped with moisture, "is my hiding place."

He pointed to the cave cut out of the bank and drew her in.

"You can see everything from here," she said, wonder filling her voice. "It's a panoramic view of the entire lake."

"Well, not the entire lake." He grinned. "But you can see a lot. Years ago I used to come here to pray."

"Not anymore?" Olivia's voice held no condemnation.

"Let's just say I haven't done it in a while." He gazed past the shoreline, past the docks, across the water where mist rose heavenward. He turned his head, smiled at her. "I guess it's time to revive the tradition, huh?"

She nodded.

They sat in silence, each busy with their own thoughts. When Olivia shivered, he put his arm around her shoulders and drew her close against his side.

"We should go back to the cottage."

"No." She slipped her hand into his and squeezed. "This is the perfect place to pray for Emily. Do you mind?"

Reese shook his head, watched her lashes drift down. While she spoke, he studied the night sky, amazed by the simplicity of her prayer.

"Father God, we pray for Emily tonight. You know her situation, You knew before we did. You also know the way to help her. Please show us what to do and please protect Emily. Keep her safe. Help her to remember to turn to You for You are our God, our healer and our protector. Amen."

Reese added his own silent amen, unable to ignore the loving tenderness with which Olivia had prayed about Emily. He added his own silent request that Olivia not be hurt by the young girl or her brother.

"Olivia?"

"Yes?" She smiled at him, that wide, generous smile that squeezed his heart into mush. When he didn't speak, her smile faltered. "What's wrong, Reese?"

"Nothing." He almost changed his mind, but then he remembered the promise he made to God, to trust. He put his other hand over hers and held on. "Would you mind praying for me?" he asked. "Specifically for the Chicago situation?"

Her face lit up, her eyes shone with joy.

"I'd love to." She grinned, a cheeky little smirk. "Actually I have been praying for you for a while. And the twins."

This time it was she who stared out over the now white-capped lake. Her prayer was to the point, her closing clear and confident.

Reese blinked the moisture away from his eyes, holding her hands as if they were an anchor.

"Thank you," he whispered.

Olivia leaned forward and brushed her lips against his.

"You're welcome," she said quietly and drew back. "Thank you for showing me your hiding place. I can understand why you'd come here to seek God. It's the perfect place to listen and hear His voice."

"I should've come here more often," he said, noting the tiny shiver she tried to hide. "I think that's all the sightseeing we should do tonight. Ready to go?" Reese rose, drew her upright beside him. "I'm very glad you're here, Olivia."

"So am I."

As they hurried back to the cottage, Reese knew his toughest challenge lay ahead to forcing the family to rethink the future. But back at the cottage, everyone else had retired. In the kitchen, on the counter, lay a note.

"Winifred. She phoned. She's thinking about us." Reese showed the paper to Olivia. "I'm running out of time to fulfill her Chicago dream."

Olivia touched his shoulder.

"Trust, remember? He has all the answers." She brushed her lips against his cheek. "Good night, Reese."

She was gone so quickly he never had the chance to respond.

Chapter Twelve

"I think you'd better give up, Reese." Olivia relaxed in the water, allowing her life jacket to buoy her up. "Obviously I am not water-ski material."

"Anybody can water-ski," he insisted, smoothing her hair from her face. "You just have to get the hang of it. Try again, Olivia."

He signaled Sara and Katie to come back around in the boat. They did, but when they got near enough, Sara shook her head.

"She's too tired now, Reese. Let her relax. Olivia can try again tomorrow."

"Thank you, Sara. I owe you big-time." Relieved, Olivia slid her feet out of her skies, undid her life jacket, swung it over one arm and began stroking toward shore. It felt great to stretch out muscles that had been tense for so long.

Sunday morning had started out great. The open-air worship service followed by a potluck lunch seemed the perfect beginning to another day at the lake. Only she hadn't reckoned on two hours of trying to master skiing on water.

"I pushed too hard, didn't I?" Reese paddled along beside her until she could stand up, then he took her life jacket. "Want to dunk me?"

"As tempting as that is, I am simply too tired." It took every effort to stagger toward her towel and the area where Emily, the twins and Reese's father played on the beach.

Olivia wrapped the thick, thirsty cotton around her body and sank into the beach chair, reveling in the warmth of the sand against her toes. She tilted her head back and shut her eyes, allowing the sun to chase away her stress.

"Are you okay?"

She lifted one eyelid, nodded at him.

"I will survive, though waterskiing is more draining than any day at Byways."

Emily giggled. "I didn't think it was that hard."

"You are younger. One day you will understand." Olivia looked at Reese. "You know the twins and Emily are itching to go. Why don't you take them? I'll rest up for our sailing event, which I assume will follow later."

"Yes, it will." He looked to his father. "Dad, can you spot for me? Sara's gone to help Cade with something and Katie said she has a date."

"As do I. Sorry, son. Your mother needs my help sorting out the storage shed. She promised chocolate cake as a reward, and you know my theory on chocolate."

"I don't." Olivia looked to Reese for an answer.

"You can never have enough chocolate." he recited. "Honestly, Dad, when are you going to get over that sweet tooth?"

"Never." His dad rose, folded his beach chair and waved. "I haven't decided whether or not to share my cake with you, son, so be nice to me." He grinned. "By the way, your grandmother's surgery is scheduled. Next week." He left.

"That's good, I think." Reese frowned.

"Maybe next time your grandmother will spot for you," Olivia teased.

"Unlikely." Reese flopped down on the sand beside her. "Grandmother loves the cottage because it brings the family together. But she likes her water in a glass or a bathtub."

"I guess I'm spotting." At least she'd brought a warm hoodie down to the beach. When Olivia put it on, her energy began to return.

"Is it our turn now, Daddy?" Brett shifted impatiently from one foot to the other, crushing the sand castle his grandfather had painstakingly erected. "I've been waiting a long time," he reminded.

"My fault," Olivia muttered.

"Nobody's fault," Reese corrected. "It wasn't a test."

"Well, it felt like one." She didn't think anyone had heard her, but Emily's snicker and Reese's frown told her differently. "Okay, I'm the spotter. What is Emily going to do?"

"What Emily always does." Reese held out his hand.

Olivia allowed him to draw her upright.

"Emily is going to help the boys get started on the skis. Then she's going to take her turn. Right, Em?"

"Right, Mr. W. I love waterskiing." Emily turned a handstand on the sand just to prove it then quickly straightened her beach shirt to cover the massive bruise on her thigh. "I fell off my bike," she said before racing away.

Fell—on the *front* of her thigh? Olivia began packing up.

"Leave what you want. No one will bother it."

"Olivia!" Sara raced toward them, her hair streaming out behind. She stopped to regain her breath before explaining, "You had a phone call. A man named—" she checked the paper she was holding then held it out. "Noslen? I think that was how he pronounced it." She paused, one eyebrow tilted.

"I don't recognize the name." Olivia frowned. "What did he want?"

"He said you had talked about interviews. Something about New York and a three-year anniversary. A glance at the past is how he phrased it." Sara shrugged. "Anyway, he wants to meet with you. Is it about Byways?"

"I haven't been there for three years." Olivia forced herself to remain calm as she concentrated on the name Sara had scribbled on the paper. Noslen. *Nelson spelled backwards.* He'd been watching her design word puzzles last week at Byways.

Olivia's heart pounded so loud she felt faint.

Nelson was letting her know that he was watching. If she tried to take Emily to the police, tried to get her to talk, Nelson would reveal everything he knew or thought he knew about Olivia's past. Then the misery she'd worked so hard to put behind her would start all over again.

Olivia couldn't, wouldn't allow that. Because this time it would be much worse. This time the news hounds and scandal mongers would have an even bigger story when they linked her to the Woodwards. The family's private lives, Winifred's health issues, Taylor's tragic death and the darling twins—all of it would be raked over, probed and scoured as food for the tabloids. They'd hone in on Byways, too.

That's how it always happened. Someone or something else got dragged into her mess because it made their stories more saleable.

"Olivia?" Reese searched her face. "You're white. Who is this guy? Is there something wrong with him?"

"Wrong with him?" She forced a laugh. "Yes, a lot and if I never see him, it will be too soon. But I'm not going to dwell on that now. This is a holiday weekend. *My* holiday weekend. Mr. Noslen will just have to wait." She shoved the note in her beach bag and slung it over one shoulder. "Race you to the boat, guys."

Olivia ran as if chased by monstrous hounds, which was exactly what this threat felt like. Once she was in the boat and Reese was towing Brady, she pulled down her sunglasses to hide her scan of the beach.

Nothing.

She had just begun to relax when she saw him, leaning against a tree, licking an ice cream cone. The boat turned. She had to swivel around, readjust her focus. Nelson was gone.

But she didn't need to see him again because his warning had worked. There was no way Olivia would do anything to jeopardize Reese or his family.

"That should tire them out. Olivia, can you dig out life jackets for the boys? They'll ride with us while Emily takes her turn."

Emily. *Oh Lord, what am I supposed to do about Emily?*

Olivia was here physically. But mentally, Reese was certain her thoughts were not on the dancing fire they'd gathered around, though she'd been staring into it for an hour.

"You're very good on the guitar, Emily." Katie smiled, slid one hand down the shiny length of Emily's hair. "Do you think you can play that song about God being so good?"

"I'll try." She began plucking out the chords.

The boys' off-key singing provided good cover. Reese nudged Olivia.

"Are you okay?" She would say she was fine. He knew that.

Reese also knew she wasn't. Something about that message this afternoon had shaken her badly enough that she'd spent their hour on his sailboat trying to pretend she wasn't studying the shoreline.

"Of course. I haven't sung the song in a long time now." She grinned. "Maybe that's a good thing."

"Why?"

"Have you ever heard me sing?"

He shook his head.

"Then you have a lot to be thankful for."

"You're right about that," he said, moving his gaze from person to person until he completed the circle of family that had gathered around. "I am very thankful for all of them. And you."

"Me? What do I have to do with this?"

Reese didn't answer. He couldn't stop staring at her, at the way the fire accented and burnished highlights in her hair. And he couldn't stop wondering at the sense of completeness he felt whenever Olivia was around. Couldn't stop marveling at the way the boys seemed naturally drawn to her, cuddling against her side with abandonment.

Most of all, he couldn't stop thanking God for bringing her into his life. All of this, and he would have missed it, had it not been for Olivia and her insistence that he find a way to learn trust in God.

"Have you had a chance to talk to the family about Chicago yet?"

"No." Reese felt for her hand, meshed his fingers into hers. "It's weird," he said softly so they wouldn't disturb the others who seemed totally involved in singing. "I've tried several times. Before dinner I suggested we have a meeting tonight. They vetoed it. It's as if they don't want to talk about it. As if everyone needs a little bit of freedom from everything connected to W by W."

"Hmm." Olivia nudged him with her elbow. "Now what?"

"I'm going to give them the time and space. If it feels right, I'll broach the subject. Otherwise I'll leave things for now. We're all nervous about Granny Win's surgery."

"Which is completely understandable." Olivia inclined her head sideways. "Look around."

Katie sang along with the others, but she kept her eyes closed, her head tilted slightly upward. Her smile transformed her face. When he told her, she would lose that blissful look. She would put aside her own wants and needs and turn her focus entirely on the company, as she always did. Katie was as devoted to Weddings by Woodwards as Winifred and one day she'd take over as CEO. How would losing Chicago affect her hopes and dreams?

Reese moved on to Sara. Her work gave them a way to reach out to the hurt and the wanting. She transformed people, helped fulfill dreams almost abandoned. Fiona made sure no dream was ever too big for Woodwards. Her grandiose designs and ability to imagine pushed far beyond mediocrity. His father saw beneath the pomp and fuss to the heart of each wedding. He garnished them with flowers as individual as each bride and groom. Katie's heart lay in management, overseeing everything with skill and grace.

Each of them had so much to lose. Reese's inability to get the Garver property could cost his family dearly.

"Maybe you could talk to them tomorrow, just before everyone leaves. Or wait until—Reese?"

"I have two weeks left. If, by Friday morning of next week, I haven't found a solution, I'll push for a decision. By then we'll know Gran's situation." He saw the disapproval darkening Olivia's eyes. "You don't agree."

"It's not right for you to carry this all on your own."

"I'm not on my own," he insisted as Cade and Sara left the group and disappeared down the beach hand in hand. "Don't you remember? God is on my side."

"So am I, Reese."

It was nice to hear. But Reese didn't miss the furtive look she cast into the bushes as they followed the path back to the cottage, each of them carrying a sleeping boy.

Olivia was afraid. And it had something to do with her past.

Maybe tomorrow they would get five minutes

alone on the sailboat and he could reassure her as she had reassured him. Reese sincerely hoped she would finally begin to trust him because his heart had begun to sing one song—Olivia Hastings.

"I had a wonderful time, Reese." It sounded like a duty thank-you, and Olivia didn't mean it that way. But neither could she give him the answers he'd asked for. "Thank you for inviting me. I just wish we'd had enough time to go for that sail this morning."

She was talking to the air. Or at least, that's how it seemed. They stood outside, the children asleep in the backseat, worn out by a weekend of sun, sand and laughter. Reese was angry.

"I don't understand why you won't tell me about this Noslen fellow. I could help you." Something about that name bugged him—as if he should recognize it.

"How?"

"By talking to him or taking the interview myself."

"No!" Olivia controlled her voice. "You can't talk to anyone. If someone comes to see you, promise me you'll send him away with no comment."

"But why?" Anger and hurt mingled in his question.

"Because this isn't about Byways," she blurted then wished she'd kept silent.

"Maybe you'd better tell me what it is about, Olivia." Reese's hands fisted, his voice tightened.

"If this guy is some kind of threat, if he's trying to come after you—"

"Leave it alone, Reese," she begged. "Don't get involved."

"I thought I was involved, Olivia. I thought we meant something to each other, that we had begun to share our lives, our problems, something." His harsh laugh hurt her. "But I guess I'm the only one sharing here, right?"

"It isn't like that, Reese," she whispered, glancing over one shoulder to be sure they hadn't disturbed the children.

"Isn't it? How would I know? You refuse to tell me anything." His voice tightened. "You won't let me intervene with Nelson though you insist he's terrorized that girl." He jerked his thumb toward a sleeping Emily. "You won't tell me anything about your past. And you won't tell me why this Noslen guy has you living in fear."

"I'm not—"

"You are, Olivia. You have been constantly on edge ever since Sara brought that message. Do you think I don't see you peering into the bushes, scouring the beach, scanning the cars?"

"There's nothing wrong with being careful," she muttered, shamed by her own cowardice.

Reese hadn't lived through that horrible media frenzy. He couldn't know how it felt to have nothing secret, nothing private, nothing you could treasure or mourn over without somebody plastering it all over page nine.

"There's nothing wrong with sharing, either. Or trying to help." The hurt tone in his voice transmitted clearly. "You tell me to trust God, to trust you, but you don't, *won't* trust me enough to tell me what's going on."

For a few precious weeks she'd thought she could start over, build a new life. But Nelson would ruin it, she knew that now. Now it was time to make sure Reese didn't get involved in her disaster.

"Stay out of it, Reese. There is nothing you can do."

He studied her for a moment then, finally, nodded. "I won't ask again, Olivia."

They climbed in the car. The rest of the drive was silent. Olivia tried to come up with a thousand ways to break the silence, but it was better this way. Better for Emily, better for Byways, and certainly better for her.

Reese pulled up in front of the address she'd given him.

"Nice house." He climbed out of the car before she could answer. The kids awakened, but he told them to stay put and walked around to the trunk to retrieve her luggage. He insisted on carrying it to the front door.

"Thank you for everything," she said sincerely.

"Forget that. I need to say something."

She inclined her head, waiting.

"I care about you, Olivia," he said quietly, resting one hand on her shoulder. "I care about you more than I thought I could care about a woman again." He smiled sadly. "I told my grandmother that a couple of weeks ago. Do you know what she said?"

Olivia slowly shook her head, afraid yet desperate to hear more.

"Grandmother gave me some very good advice. She told me that the starting place for any two people was sharing. She was talking about our faith differences, but her comment is valid all the same." Now both hands rested on her shoulders as he waited for her to look at him.

"Don't," she whispered.

"I have to say this because I'm in love with you." His eyes brightened as if this was the first time he'd admitted the truth to himself. Just as quickly, vitality drained away. "I want to explore the future with you, Olivia. I want it all. The sharing, the caring, the honesty even when it hurts. I need that—for myself and as a witness to the boys so they can see what real love is all about."

"I'm sorry."

Reese pressed a finger against her lips.

"I'm not," he whispered. "Because I can wait for you, Olivia. I trust you. Please trust me."

He kissed her on the lips once, hard, and then he was gone, pulling away from the curb before she could say the words that would betray her.

I love you, too, Reese.

She'd call him, tell him everything he wanted to know. Love didn't come so easily that when God blessed you with it a second time, you could throw it away.

Olivia opened the door eagerly, ready to race to the phone. Her foot slipped. She glanced down. Someone had slid a paper through the letter slot.

Last warning. Stay out of my business or I'll get into yours. N.

Hope died as Olivia grasped the paper in her fingers and squeezed it into a ball. An envelope lay nearby. Inside were copies of new stories, all of them from her past.

Nelson knew it all.

The phone rang.

"I trust you understand me."

"Why are you doing this, Nelson?"

"Because you won't mind your own business." He snickered. "It's been a while since you and Trevor appeared in publications. And sweet little Anika. Don't you think it's time the people of Denver got to know your daughter?"

"Threatening people is illegal, Nelson."

"That wasn't a threat. It was a promise. Stay away from Emily or I'll spread the story you're so anxious to keep quiet."

Olivia slammed down the phone. Then she reached for the articles and tore the hated things to shreds, dragged in her luggage and shut the door with her foot. She stood in the stillness and absorbed the room she'd thought so beautiful. But it was just a room in another house. It couldn't hold her, soothe her. Love her.

Olivia ignored the flash of the answering machine, the laundry that needed doing and the myriad jobs that simply occupied time. Instead she walked through the house and opened the doors onto the patio. The cushioned furniture she chosen so carefully stood waiting and she collapsed onto a chaise, pouring out her heart to her Father.

"Help me, Lord God."

Chapter Thirteen

It was Wednesday. Olivia double-checked her calendar. Emily hadn't been to Byways since returning from the lake on Monday, and Olivia was worried.

Yesterday, in front of the staff, she'd finally asked Nelson where his sister was. His fatuous smile grew with his answer.

"Emily is in school now, Olivia. You know that. She simply doesn't have time to hang around here anymore."

It was a good answer, but not good enough.

So today, with Casey nearby, Olivia had queried Nelson once more, and again he put her off with some excuse about Emily's busyness.

"I understand she has things to do, but Emily was particularly interested in guitar lessons." Olivia ignored his sniff of disgust. "I know she intended to be here this afternoon for her first class."

"I don't think Emily is going to have time for guitar lessons. Perhaps you should concentrate your efforts on the children we are here to serve," he said with a self-righteous air that made Olivia grit her teeth.

That smile killed her poise.

"Where is your sister, Nelson?"

"Emily is none of your business. I am her guardian. Remember that."

"Guardianship can be changed," Olivia hissed.

He turned on her like a feral animal, teeth bared.

"Do you require another reminder of what can happen with your past, Mrs. *Hastings?*"

Furious at herself for weakening under his threats, and at him for daring to threaten her, Olivia stepped nearer until she was almost nose to nose.

"Be careful what you say to me, Nelson. I will only be pushed so far."

"Ready to tell all, are we?" He smiled. "I'll alert the media."

Olivia shuddered, but held her ground. "I will not let you hurt Emily."

"You will mind your own business. Or you know what will happen." He handed her a piece of paper, an article that detailed her past and present, including Reese, the twins and Winifred. "I can have this in tonight's paper," he warned before he stalked away.

Olivia's worry over his threat grew as she read the exposé. But she could not suppress her concern about

Emily. So she dialed Emily's cell phone number, but Emily did not answer. Twice Olivia picked up the phone to call Reese, and twice she hung up when she realized she'd have to tell him everything. He must now be frantic about Winifred's impending operation. She didn't want to add to his concerns.

But because her worries about Emily would not abate, Olivia rushed through work and hurried home to change. With no answer on the cell, Olivia finally called the Kirsch house. But Nelson insisted Emily was at her guitar lesson. Knowing this was untrue, Olivia began scouring the streets in search of a young girl who had become like a daughter. She found no one.

Nancy called to say a New York reporter was on his way to Denver.

Olivia took the matter to her Father. On Thursday she visited the local schools to introduce herself and Byways's programs to any of the students who didn't already know. Afterward she lingered in the hallways, questioned Sylvia, the girl who'd befriended Emily. By one o'clock in the afternoon Olivia finally had a clue.

She'd deliberately selected worn jeans, an old T-shirt and a pair of sneakers for work this morning. Now she slung on a tired leather jacket that had seen better days and braved the stares and whispers that followed her into a teenage hangout in the roughest part of town.

It took less than five minutes to locate Emily

huddling behind her backpack in a corner, trying to ignore the attentions of a man ten years older than she was.

"Emily." Olivia wrapped her arms around young girl and held her tight as tears of joy mixed with relief. "Oh, Emily, I am so glad I found you. I've been searching and—" The words died on her lips. "Oh, Emily."

Disfigured by bruising, cuts and swelling, Emily drew back and hugged her midriff.

"Sweetheart, what's wrong? Are you hurt? Inside, I mean?"

"Go away." Tears rolled down her cheeks, but Emily stepped backward and shook her head. "You have to go away," she enunciated through lips swollen twice their normal size.

Olivia shook her head.

"No, Emily. I am not leaving you. Nelson is not going to get the chance to do this to you again. Ever. Do you understand me?"

"He'll hurt you." Fear swelled in her eyes. "He knows things about you."

"It doesn't matter." She held out her hand. "Come on, sweetie. Let's get you to a hospital."

"No!" Emily pressed against the wall, shaking her head slowly from side to side. "He said, he said—" A hiccup choked off her words.

"It doesn't matter what he said. I won't let him hurt you, Emily. You can trust me. I promise." Still, Emily backed away. Olivia searched for a way to convince her. "The only way Nelson could hurt me is if he hurts you."

"He pays guys to do stuff. He got them to break into your office so it wouldn't look like it was him who really wanted a phone number you had. Also to scare you. He likes that."

"It doesn't matter," Olivia said, shaking her head. "Do you know why, Emily?"

Emily shook her head from side to side, her eyes as wide as her swollen lids would allow.

"Because I have a protector. I put my faith in God, Emily. Remember what you learned in your class at church? God is bigger than Nelson, bigger than Nelson's friends. He's big enough to protect you and me and everyone else who trusts in Him."

"I guess," Emily murmured.

"I know." Olivia coaxed her to sit down and ordered a drink for both of them. "You can't go back to that house, Emily. Not while he's there. And you certainly can't go back to stay."

"But where will I live?" Fat tears dripped down her purpling cheeks. "I don't think I can stay on the street another night, Olivia. I was so scared last night."

"Why didn't you call me? You know I would have come," she reminded quietly, not wanting to add to the girl's pain, but needing to know. "Nelson can't hurt me, Emily, so don't worry about protecting me. I'm an adult and I know how to protect myself. There is no way I intend to ever let him hurt you again."

"But why?" Emily whispered, pressing back into the seat as a burly man approached their table. She hissed out a breath of sheer relief when he stopped at the next one. "Why me, Olivia? I'm nothing to you."

"Are you kidding me?" Olivia shook her head back to dispel her own tears. "You, my dear Emily, are as precious to me as my own daughter—would be," she added quickly. "I've watched you grow and change. I've seen you protect the twins, help them and their dad without complaining. I've been so proud to watch you work at Byways. You're right here." She tapped her chest. "You're part of my heart, Emily."

"Really?" Emily stared. "Truly?"

"Really, truly, absolutely, positively certain." Olivia grinned. "If you can find the courage to tell the police what Nelson did to you, then I intend to ask them if you can come home with me."

"To your place?" Emily gaped, but then she was back to being a scared little girl again. "For how long?"

"For as long as you want, for as long as the authorities will let you. I need a roommate in that big house."

"I'd like that," Emily said, suddenly shy.

"I'd like it, too. But first I need to apologize to you."

"To me?" Confusion spread across the battered face. "Why?"

"Because I'm partly to blame for what happened to you."

"No! You didn't do anything to me." Emily's voice was fierce. "All you did was try to help me."

"Oh, sweetie." Olivia wanted to hug her, but she was afraid she'd hurt her. "I love you for saying that, but the truth is, I've suspected Nelson has been abusing you verbally for quite some time. I never realized it had gone this far."

"I didn't want you to know."

"You have nothing to be ashamed about! I should have done something earlier and I will never forgive myself for letting things get this bad."

"Olivia, it's not your fault. He never hit me before. This time when he did, I was too scared. All I could do was run away." Emily's sobs interspersed her words. "I'm still scared, but I'm going to talk to the police. I want to be like you, strong enough to stand up when things are wrong. I'm not going to let Nelson hurt anyone else." She took another sip of her drink, then eased out of her seat. "Let's go."

They walked outside, arm in arm. Olivia opened her car door then paused, trying to get past the emotion that filled her.

"Can I just take a moment to tell you how proud I am of you, Emily? It takes a strong person to stand up for themselves, but it takes true grit and spirit to stand up for someone else. I think you're one of the strongest girls I've ever met."

Emily sat a little straighter in her seat. And when they arrived at the police station she calmly but firmly answered every question. When they wanted photos, she allowed them, her voice wobbling only for a moment before she glanced at Olivia.

At the hospital she stayed firm while the doctors examined her and treated her injuries. When they asked, she told them exactly how each one had occurred. They returned to the police station where two detectives assured Emily that they had her brother in custody and that he would not be allowed to see her or communicate with her.

"The courts don't like men who beat children," the sergeant explained. "With all the information you've given us, it will be simple to get a conviction. He will be in prison for a long time."

"I didn't want him to be hurt," Emily whispered, her face pale.

"Honey, when the twins disobey, Reese disciplines them, right?" Emily nodded. "Well, it's the same for adults. I warned Nelson, but he wouldn't stop. Now he will be punished. That isn't your fault. You've done the right thing."

When the police had confirmed Olivia's credentials and learned of her past standing with the court, they assured child services that Emily would be well taken care of. Emily would be allowed to stay with Olivia for the time being.

The two hugged each other.

"Let's go home, Emily."

Emily would need to talk later, but for now it was enough that she was safe.

Their seat belts were barely locked when Olivia's cell phone rang.

"Reese? You'll never believe—" She listened for a moment. "I'll be there as quick as I can. Pray, Reese. I will, too. And keep trusting God." She hung up slowly.

"What's wrong?"

"The twins are missing. They were out at Cade and Sara's ranch for the day. Reese said they ran away. He also said there's a storm on the way."

"Oh, no." Emily grabbed her hand. "We have to go out there. Now. I have to help. Maybe I can find them."

"Honey, you're in no shape to go searching. Especially with a storm approaching." Olivia tamped down her own worries.

Emily sat up straight, her face intent.

"I love Brett and Brady. If there's a way I can help, I'm going to do it. If you won't drive me, I'll hitch-hike."

Pride bloomed inside Olivia. This girl deserved more credit than Nelson ever gave her.

"Okay, then. We're going. Have you got a jacket in that backpack?"

"Yes. And some snacks. Nelson's going to be mad. He buys them for his hiking trips into the mountains."

"I doubt he'll have to worry about hiking for a while," Olivia muttered as she steered toward the ranch. "Remember how they taught us to pray, Emily?"

"Yes." Emily grinned. "I'm praying. But I think that God has the twins hidden some place special so they're protected."

Olivia grimaced. Trust the hole in her faith to be illuminated by a child. Here she was preaching faith to Reese and she was the one who hadn't trusted God to protect her when Nelson made his threats. Her stupidity about the past resurfacing was as stupid as Reese's stubborn refusal to let his family share his burden about Chicago.

It was well past time, Olivia knew, that she gave her whole situation to God and let him handle it. It was obvious to her now that as soon as Nelson had the opportunity he would spread her past to anyone who cared to listen, if he hadn't already. Casey said she'd chased away two reporters from New York this morning.

It would start again soon. The microphones shoved in her face, the endless questions, the ringing phone at four in the morning. Surely she'd have time to tell Reese the truth once the twins were found.

Olivia hoped. No way did she want the Woodwards unprepared for the onslaught of media she expected.

"Protect them, Father. Hold them in the safety of Your hand."

Don't take those children, she wanted to beg.

But trust had to be complete and Olivia had to turn it over to the One who loved the twins far more than she.

Chapter Fourteen

"I have to do something!" Reese paced Sara's kitchen to keep himself from exploding. "I can't wait."

"Yes, you can. You can wait and pray," Olivia said from the doorway. She walked over to him and wrapped her arms around his waist. "We all can."

His hands automatically slid up her back, drawing her nearer as he inhaled her sweet fragrance.

"Olivia. I'm so glad you came."

"Nothing could keep me away. Or Emily," she whispered.

He glanced across the room, felt his knees weaken at the condition of Emily's face.

"Nelson," he guessed.

"Yes, but he's in jail. Emily insisted on coming to help." She stepped away, but her hand slid into his. "Where do we start?"

"We're waiting for the sheriff. Sara and Cade have begun searching some of the outbuildings, but it's so slow." He dragged a hand through his hair. "I'm scared, Olivia. Really scared. They're so small. Anything could happen."

"But it won't because God is their protector. Trust, Reese."

"I'm trying." He closed his eyes. "It's my fault they ran away."

"No," Olivia murmured, but he shook his head.

"Yes. I had a telephone conference planned with Mrs. Garvin. I was racing to get them ready for Sara to pick up. They kept fooling around, playing their silly dinosaur games." The idea that he might never hear those giggles again choked off his words. "I yelled at them, Olivia. I let work and all its inherent problems take precedence over my kids."

"No." She touched his cheek, forced him to look into her lovely eyes. "You are a parent. We're allowed to make mistakes once in a while."

We? He frowned.

"I'll explain later. For now, let's think about the twins. You've done your best for those boys, Reese, but you can't protect them now. Only God can. Let's ask Him to help."

"Excellent idea, Olivia." Fiona followed Thomas inside and let the door slam shut as she led in prayer.

"Thank you, Mom." Reese hugged her, but the urge to do something could not be suppressed. "I wish Cade and Sara would check in," he muttered.

"Wow, it's nasty out there." Katie stepped into the house. "Anything yet?"

Reese shook his head, but stopped when he noticed Emily heading outside. Olivia followed. He trailed behind, curiosity rising.

"Where are you going, Em? Olivia?"

"There's a special place they like to hide in the horse arena," the girl whispered nervously, peeking at him fearfully as everyone's attention centered on them. "Maybe they're there."

"Go," he said. And to Olivia, "Will you go with her? Please? I need to wait for the sheriff."

She nodded and they hurried away.

Inside, Reese glanced around the room, suddenly aware that no matter how hard he worked, how carefully he tried to prevent bad things from happening, he could, in the end, offer very little security to the ones he loved the most.

It had been simpler when the twins were small and seldom left the house, but soon they'd be involved in their school programs. That would bring numerous opportunities for risk that he would have no control over.

His brother, Donovan, was in Europe. Reese held his power of attorney, but that did not mean he could prevent Donovan from being hit by a car or any of the other horrible things that filled the news.

The only security he had lay in his trust in God. From God came the gifts of his children, the joys of a family he had not been born into, and the unexpected love for a woman who had helped resurrect his faith.

In the end, all Reese had was his faith, and a battered but sturdy fragment of trust in God to work things out.

"They're not there," Emily said through tears. "I was so sure…"

"Don't worry, Emily." Fiona patted her shoulder. "The Bible says God made each of us, all the delicate inner parts of our bodies and knit them together in our mother's womb. He didn't go to all that trouble to lose Brett and Brady."

The rest of the family followed her example, trying to encourage each other with Biblical verses proclaiming God's ability to protect.

"Wait a minute!" Emily's voice rang out above them all. "Wait."

"What is it, Em?"

Emily stared at Olivia.

"I didn't mean to snoop," she whispered. "I was afraid of Nelson. I was afraid that he'd do something horrible and I was so scared…"

"It doesn't matter. Whatever it was, it doesn't matter," Olivia soothed. "Just tell us what happened."

"When I was telling the twins their bedtime story that last night at the lake," she said to Fiona who nodded, urging her to continue. "They started asking about their mom, like where she was and what she was doing." She stared at Olivia. "They were upset and I couldn't think what to tell them. Then I remembered what I'd seen on Nelson's desk. I'm so sorry."

Reese didn't understand what this was about, but

he knew time was not on their side. Already the wind was howling outside, churning icy bits of sleet all over the land. The boys had been wearing summer clothes when Sara picked them up. In this weather—

"Go on, Emily." Olivia alone seemed to understand what was holding the girl back. She smiled, nodded. "It's all right."

Emily nodded back. She inhaled, exhaled slowly.

"I told them their mom was in heaven looking after a little girl named Anika. Olivia's daughter," she whispered when no one seemed to understand.

"You have a daughter?" Reese couldn't conceive of why she would hide such a thing, but he was afraid to find out now, afraid to delay finding his kids.

"Had." Her wistful smile faltered. "I'll explain later. Go on, Emily."

"Nelson has piles of papers about you, about how you had a husband and a little girl and how they died. I'm sorry."

Trevor, the man who loved coffee. Reese knew it as surely as his own name.

"Keep going," Olivia urged.

"Well, the twins kept asking me about heaven, what it was like." Emily frowned. "I told them what I heard at church, but they couldn't seem to understand. Brett thought it sounded like heaven was a playground and Brady was positive it was a candy store."

"Those two." Thomas's chuckles brought Emily's smile.

"Yeah." Emily grinned. "Anyway, I tried to think of something else, so they'd understand, you know?"

"You've always tried to help them understand, Emily." Reese patted her shoulder. "You did fine."

"I remembered when they got wet that afternoon your sister got married. I told them heaven was kind of like that valley with pretty flowers and stuff. Where no one could make you do things you didn't want to."

"Oh, dear Lord." Fiona clapped a hand over her mouth.

Reese couldn't say anything. Fear choked off his breath.

"You think they went to the valley?" Olivia squeezed his hand for encouragement. "You think they went there to look for their mother?"

"Yes." Emily nodded, tears filling her eyes. "They saw a little building down there. They called it a hidey-house. They were always telling me how much they wanted a mom. Not because they don't love you," she whispered to Reese. "Because they think you're lonely, that you need someone to talk to, like they have each other."

"I know what you mean, Emily." Brett and Brady had said something of the sort to him this morning. But Reese had cut them off because he was so busy proving himself he'd forgotten he was a father first and foremost.

"It's my fault, because of what I said," Emily mourned. "They wouldn't have thought of it if it wasn't for me."

Trust. Now was the time.

I trust You with their lives, Father.

"Emily." He knelt in front of her and gently touched a tissue to her cheeks. "You are the best sitter my sons ever had. They love and adore you as much as if you were their sister. You tried to make them understand about heaven just the way a sister would. Thank you. Now, do you want to come help me get them?"

"Oh, yes," she said eagerly.

"How?" Olivia asked.

"This is a ranch. They have horses here." He grinned at Cade and Sara, who had walked in a few moments earlier. "Don't you?"

"Already saddled, Bro. Ready to start a search. Rescue package and extra blankets included." Sara stood on tiptoes and kissed his cheek. "Go get them."

"I'll go with you," Cade offered.

"You sure? I know you've been working long hours for roundup."

"I know this place better than anyone, Reese." Cade grinned. "Besides, when it's family, it's a labor of love."

"That's why I married him." Sara beamed.

Cade kissed her cheek. "Be praying," he said.

"We all will," Fiona assured him. "Get some heavy coats on now."

Reese glanced at Olivia.

"Want to come?"

"Try and keep me away, Reese Woodward." She

grinned. "I intend to point out to you exactly how trustworthy our Lord is."

"You go, girl." Katie cheered with a grin. She made sure they were suitably clothed then shooed them out the door. "I'll speak to the sheriff."

"Are you okay to ride, Emily?" Reese helped Olivia mount.

"Try and stop me." She gave Olivia a thumbs-up then winced as Reese helped her into her saddle. "I'm not going to be jumping on the trampoline for a while."

"She won't make the mistake of not trusting God again," Olivia said. She smiled. "Neither will I."

Reese took her hand, pressed his lips to her knuckles.

"You better have a really good explanation for keeping secrets from me, lady." He waited for her smile. "Let's go."

Reese led the way into the darkening world as his heart silently offered the same prayer a man had prayed centuries earlier.

Lord, I believe. Help my unbelief.

The bitter wind, the icy cold, the dampness that seeped through her extrathick coat—Olivia couldn't imagine how two children could last long in such conditions. But that didn't stop her prayers.

"There's the shed." Cade led the way, his horse nimbly avoiding picky edges and marshy spots not easily discernable. He slung out of his seat and tethered the horse to a tree, then helped Emily. "Slowly, easily. We don't want to frighten them."

Reese dismounted and Olivia followed. She grasped his hand as they moved forward together. Cade opened the door and they entered.

"Thank you, Lord," Reese whispered.

Olivia echoed the sentiment as the frightened father knelt between his sons and checked their breathing.

"They're asleep," he whispered in amazement.

"Daddy?" Brett's eyelashes flickered open. He sat up, wrapped his arms around his father's neck. "Hi, Daddy. Brady an' me couldn't find our mom. She must be really busy looking after Olivia's little girl, don't you think?"

"Not too busy." Brady also sat up. "'Cause she has God to help her." He grinned. "Right, Emily?"

"Right." Emily hugged each of them, but the mother in her would not be silenced. "You guys shouldn't have come here alone. There's a big storm on."

"That's why we came in here," Brady told her.

"We didn't go near the water, Uncle Cade." Brett scrunched up his face. "Only I don't like the smell of that blanket." He plucked the old tarp away.

Everyone burst out laughing. Reese gathered them in his arms and smiled at her. Olivia smiled back, but the ache in her heart wouldn't go away. She remained silent as Reese wrapped the boys in the coats Sara had sent then added blankets.

"Let's go," he said.

"Wait!" Brady broke free of his grasp and walked over to Olivia. "You don't have to worry about your little girl," he said quietly. "God likes kids. He doesn't get mad at them."

"Thank you, darling," she whispered, tears clogging her throat.

His eyes flew wide open. He turned to his twin. "Hey, Brett. Maybe Olivia could be our new mom."

"We'll talk about that and dads who get angry and a whole lot of other stuff," Reese promised. "But not till we get home. Okay?"

They agreed and together they left the little shack.

As they rode back, Olivia tried to imagine what her life would be like without this wonderful family.

She'd soon find out. As soon Nelson told the media, she would have to leave. No way would she let her scandal touch this special family.

The knowledge that they'd be safe brought both joy and sorrow.

She would be alone. Again.

Chapter Fifteen

"I'm so thankful for Emily." Reese set two big mugs of hot chocolate on the coffee table then sat down beside Olivia in front of the flickering fire. "Actually, I'm thankful for a lot of things. Emily's safe, with no permanent damage. And now she's telling the boys their bedtime stories."

"Reese? I need to explain."

"You don't have to," he said quietly. But he could see the urgency on her face. She needed to talk. "But I'll listen if you want."

"I want." Her glossy cinnamon hair curled around her face, almost hiding it.

Reese sensed she needed the privacy to say what was on her heart.

"I was married for five years, and I had a radio talk show where I counseled children. I met Trevor just after my show took off. He was kind and gentle, a pediatric surgeon. We were very happy, especially when our daughter arrived." Her eyes grew misty with remembering. "Anika was such a great kid. Intuitive, talkative, full of the giggles." A sob escaped her.

"Olivia." Reese touched her shoulder, grazed his thumb underneath her eye to wipe away the tears. "It's okay. I don't have to hear this." But the way she looked at him told him she needed to speak of the past. "I'm listening."

"She was four when she and her father were kidnapped."

The words knocked him for a loop. Kidnapped?

"It sounds crazy when I say it now, but my life really was too perfect. My radio talk show was in national syndication. Kids all across the nation were calling to talk about their problems." She shook her head. "I was so proud of my success, so delighted that finally wounded children had a place where they could speak openly about what was bothering them. And then it was gone. Stolen."

Reese ached to hold her, to erase the pain visible in her dark, expressive irises. But he remained still, and let her continue.

"I had just finished the show when he called in. Apparently his daughter had been one of the callers on my show the day before. He said I'd told her that she had the right to walk away from an abusive situation. She was killed in a hit-and-run two hours after she'd left home. He blamed me, so he kidnapped my family."

"Oh, darling. I'm sorry."

"He said five million dollars would ease his sorrow. I arranged for payment. I would've done anything to keep them safe." Olivia's voice was now flat and dull.

Reese could guess what was coming.

"He never picked up the money. The police said my husband and daughter were already dead when he called." She looked at him, eyes blazing with pain. "He said he wanted me to know how it felt to lose a child, to lose the most important thing in your life. And now I know."

Reese wrapped an arm around her shoulders and hugged her against his side as she softly sobbed.

"Was the man not caught?"

"Yes. He's in jail and he'll stay there."

"So why keep it a secret?"

"Why?" Olivia drew back, tried to smile. "My husband was the son of a senator, Reese. A very famous senator who publicly blamed me for their deaths. You cannot imagine my life when the media got hold of the story. They camped on my doorstep, they phoned constantly. They even followed me to the funeral home. I was big news in the East, a celebrity. Private pain was up for public consumption. And it did not end with the funerals. Or the trial or after it was over. I couldn't go back on the radio, I was too afraid another child might die. Because of me."

"It wasn't because of you, Olivia." Reese drew her

nearer and pressed his lips to her forehead. "That child was in pain and needed help. You gave her hope."

"I went into hiding," she murmured. "Friends helped me change my name back to my maiden name. I moved constantly from place to place, that's why my resume is so odd. I only listed about half the places I worked. And always, every single time, they found me. And ran another story." She lifted her head, stared at him. "Until I came here."

"You thought I would betray you?"

"Not after the first day." She smiled. "But I was fairly certain Nelson would. And he will, if he hasn't already."

"But why?"

"Money." The scorn she invested into that single word told him all he needed to know.

"So you have a lot of money."

"A lot," she agreed, studying his eyes. "Have you ever heard of Edward Hastings?"

"The stockbroker?" Reese gaped. "That was your grandfather?"

"Yes." Olivia nodded. "He left me everything. So did Trevor. I have a lot of money, Reese, and that makes it more difficult because money corrupts. I wanted to use it to do some good, but every time I tried, some nosy newshound connected me to that radio host in New York City who so tragically lost her husband and daughter, or who killed them, depending on the story. I couldn't let

Trevor and Anika's memories be tarnished anymore, so I hid."

Reese turned so he faced her. He rested his hands on her shoulders and looked her straight in the eye.

"Dearest Olivia, my heart aches for the pain and suffering you've gone through. If I could erase it all and give you back your loved ones I would. But I can't." He touched her forehead, traced her delicately arched brows. He followed it down her nose to her beautiful smile that could light up his world without saying a word.

"I know."

"To be perfectly honest, I'm glad you're here now because I love you, Olivia. I don't care about your money." He touched her cheek. "Give it away or lock it up in a bank or burn it. It doesn't matter to me."

"You can't say that, Reese. You don't know." She tried to explain. "They'll come around, they'll take pictures of the twins, push into your backyard, invade every ounce of privacy you have just to get their story on the front page and make the almighty buck."

"It doesn't matter."

"It doesn't?"

"Not a bit." He smiled. "You matter to me, your happiness, your problems and your heart. I have a lot to learn about families and I *can* learn, Olivia." He brushed his thumb across her lips. "Please say you'll join mine and teach me how to give and receive love."

He waited, breath suspended, for her response.

"Are you—"

"I'm asking you to marry me. Soon."

"But what about—"

"The twins and I come as a package deal. The rest of it we'll leave up to God. I trust Him, Olivia. Don't you?"

Two giggles cut off her response.

"I'm story for interrupting, but the boys have a question I can't answer." Emily drew them forward. "Two minutes," she reminded in her big sister voice. "You have two minutes and then you're going to bed. You promised, remember?"

"We promise." Brett and Brady flopped down on the floor beside them. "Daddy, is Olivia going to be our mom?"

Reese winced. If she said no now, the kids would be decimated. He should have foreseen this.

"Funny you should ask." Olivia stared at him for a moment then leaned forward and whispered in his ear.

Reese nodded. "Perfect," he told her.

"The thing is, your dad and I were just talking about that, but we have a little problem." She had the twins eating out of her hand, but Reese knew the next part was up to him.

"We want to be a family, but we need Emily to join us." He reached up a hand to the young girl and drew her into their group. "Would you mind joining our family and being a big sister to these two? You're already the daughter of our hearts."

"Are you gonna have a wedding?" Brett asked.

"Yes." Olivia studied him. "Would you like that?"

"Yeah!" Brady's eyes widened. "Hey, Emily can get that white dress she always wanted and wear it to the wedding. Girls always wear white dresses to weddings. Can't she, Daddy?"

"Absolutely," Reese agreed. "The prettiest dress we can find."

Emily was weeping, but she was also smiling as she nodded her enthusiastic agreement.

"Boy, that Sunday school teacher knew what she was talking about when she said God wants to give us the desires of our heart."

The doorbell rang.

Reese saw Olivia's blink of panic.

"Emily, would you put the boys to bed, please?" He kissed them each then grabbed Olivia's hand. "It's time to face your monster," he whispered. "Lean on me."

When he opened the door a camera snapped. Several more followed. A tall, lean, gray-haired man stepped forward, pushing an outstretched microphone out of the way.

"Reese." The man nodded before turning to her. "Miss Hastings, my name is Arthur Woodward. Winifred asked me to come. Since I own a television station, she thought I might have some ideas on how you could handle things."

"Darling Grandmother." Reese chuckled, shook the man's hand. "Even from her hospital she's still directing. We're at your mercy, Art."

Art grinned, nodded and faced the photographers.

"If any of you are interested, I have a statement here I'd like to read. It's from Winifred Woodward."

He announced the surgery she was to endure the next morning and that she expected to be back at Weddings by Woodwards in the very near future.

"She took the publicity for us," Olivia whispered. "They'll focus on her for now."

"Of course Winifred intends to handle any and all family weddings," Art answered the reporter's question with a smile. "Isn't she the queen of weddings? Now you might as well run with that because I won't release another statement until tomorrow morning. In the meantime, say a prayer for her and her family, will you?"

He ushered them inside and closed the door.

"That should do it," he said with satisfaction. "Winifred would like to see you now, if you don't mind. I'll stay with the kids."

"You're a real blessing to this family, Art. Thanks." Reese listened as Art told them of the escape route he'd prepared via the backyard.

At the hospital, Winifred lay still, her face pale but content. Olivia bent and kissed her forehead. The timeless smile flashed at them both.

"Hello, darlings."

"How long have you known who I am?" Olivia asked.

"From the moment I heard you speak," Winifred said. "I used to listen to your broadcasts every day. Such a wise woman you are. And now I'll have another granddaughter to go with my new store. Isn't God good?"

"Uh, Grandmother, about Chicago." Reese dreaded disappointing her. But at least he knew God would comfort his grandmother.

"Now, Reese." Olivia threaded her arm through his and shook her head. "Your grandmother needs to rest. Say good night."

"Good night, Grandmother. I love you."

"I love you, too, darling. Both of you." She smiled as the nurse shooed them away to join the rest of the family in the chapel.

They stayed there through the night, praying, holding each other, treasuring moments every family dreads. By dawn, talk turned to the store.

"We have to talk about Chicago," Reese began. "I can't handle it alone."

"Now?" Katie wondered. "Shouldn't we wait until we see how Grandmother—"

"Grandmother is going to be fine. We owe it to her to have this nailed down so she doesn't worry and fuss about it anymore." He drew a deep breath.

Olivia squeezed his fingers.

"Before you begin, Reese, I was wondering if Weddings by Woodwards would consider taking on a partner in your Chicago store." Olivia studied each face in turn, checking to see if anyone objected. "You see, I've been thinking of investing for my future and there's this property I'm interested in. It belongs to a woman named Garver."

"Olivia." Guilt rushed over Reese for the many times he'd laid his problems on her. "You don't have to do this."

"Can't you see how much I want that money to be used for good? Winifred can make her store a testament to God, Reese. And I can help her do it." She kissed his cheek. "I need to do this. After all, I'm going to be part of the family, aren't I?"

"Of course you are." Fiona smiled and patted her cheek. "A welcome addition. Now, here come the doctors."

"Mrs. Woodward handled the operation very well. Her prognosis is excellent. You should all go home and rest. You can visit later tonight."

They hugged and cried and kissed. Then one by one, they filed out.

Lastly, Reese led Olivia out of the hospital.

"You just agreed to marry me, you know."

"Of course I know. I'm no dummy." She returned his kiss. "About that, I've got a couple of other ideas to run past you."

"We've got the rest of our lives," he promised, folding her into his arms.

Epilogue

The bride wore an elegant cream silk suit designed by Winifred Woodward herself. The matrons and maids of honor, sisters of the groom, also wore creations by Woodward in soft heather. The junior bridesmaid, Emily, wore a specially created cream gown studded with pearls. And the ring bearers, twin sons of the groom, looked resplendent in gray suits that matched their father's.

The wedding took place at Byways, a children's center where the bride is employed. Below is a photo of the bride and groom and the announcement they made of a bequest to the Byways foundation. The couple is enjoying their honeymoon at an undisclosed location.

"Whatcha doin', Great Granny?"

"I'm reading about the wedding. Do you boys want to see a picture?"

They looked, nodded, but Emily called from the trampoline and that took precedence.

Winifred watched them leave, then scanned the rest of the paper.

A small article discussed the court case of Emily's brother and his recent incarceration. Winifred nodded her head at the term and moved to the bottom of the page.

Weddings by Woodwards Chairman Winifred Woodward announced today that Donovan Woodward, her grandson, will soon return to the company as marketing manager of the founding Weddings by Woodwards store here in Denver. Those in the know say Mrs. Woodward, senior, will soon relocate to Chicago to open a new store in that city.

"That's what you think." Winifred chuckled. She checked the caller ID on her ringing cell phone. "Hi, Art. Yes, I've read it. It's mostly factual. Dinner? I'd love it."

She said goodbye and laid down the phone, but paused a moment to close her eyes.

"I'll be talking to you about Donovan, Father. Soon."

* * *

In a beautiful house across town a husband and wife toasted each other with frosty lemonade as they basked beside the pool in autumn's unexpected warmth.

"Wouldn't you rather have gone to some exotic place?" the bride asked.

"Sweetheart, there's exotic," the groom murmured as he kissed her. "And then there's perfection. Fortunately, I know the difference."

"Mmm." Olivia lay back on her chaise. "What do you think God has planned for our future?"

"I don't know. But whatever it is, I trust Him to lead us."

"So do I."

Two stars twinkled in the evening sky.

"Good night, darlings." Olivia smiled. "I love you."

The stars seemed blaze for a second, then they receded into the heavens until she could no longer see them. Olivia relinquished her cherished loved ones into God's care.

"Are you okay?" Reese asked as he drew her upright. His arms circled her waist.

"Perfect." She tilted her head to see his face. "Did I ever demonstrate my diving prowess?"

He shook his head.

"It starts like this," she said and nudged him into the water.

"Olivia!"

"I'm coming."

A moment later Olivia dived into the water, ready to enjoy the Father's precious gift of love given a second time.

* * * * *

Dear Reader,

Hello there! Welcome back to Weddings by Woodwards—the family wedding store that plans weddings that dreams are made of. I had so much fun with the Woodward twins. And Emily—well, she's the babysitter we all want, isn't she? Families are the cement that connects us together—whether we're born into them, adopted by them or marry into them. There's nothing more special than having people who will love you in spite of everything.

Now that Reese and Olivia are happily married, I hope you'll come back to Woodwards in June for Donovan's story in A RING AND A PROMISE. Donovan expects too little of himself but Abby knows he can stretch to become the man of her dreams.

Till then I wish you a glorious spring filled with family, fun and a fresh new way of seeing our heavenly Father who never stops loving.

Blessings,

Lois
Richer

QUESTION FOR DISCUSSION

1. Today's society does not seem to put an emphasis on families. Busy lives, a fast pace, demanding careers all take their toll on parents. List ways a family can carve out special times to be together.

2. Though he became a Woodward many years before, Reese never really accepted the abundant love that was offered him by his family because he was afraid he wasn't worthy of their love. Discuss how we scorn the love God offers us, or never completely accept Him as our parent.

3. Nelson was one of those people whose beguiling smile hides their true nature. If you were Olivia, what would you have done differently? List things we might do or say to help those who are enduring tough times?

4. Reese kept his problems with the Chicago store to himself when he could have shared them with his family. Are there things for which we should never ask for help? List reasons why or why not.

5. Do you feel that a ministry like Byways would work in your community? Who are some people

you know who would benefit from it? What could you do to help such a place?

6. Abuse is an ugly subject. It's hard to prove and people often don't report it because they fear becoming involved or they feel threatened. Pretend you are Emily's father. Discuss ways you could handle Nelson.

7. In North America, children often have so many things, but they have no one who will spend time with them, lead or guide them and encourage them. We need mentors. Suggest ways you and your friends could mentor someone else without going through a formal agency.

8. Publicity and money are often tied together. Offer your thoughts on the rights of public people such as movie stars and elected officials to have their personal privacy respected. Are the tabloids a violation of those rights? Why or why not?

9. For many, God as a father figure is hard to accept. List some ways you might explain God's love to them.

10. The twins wanted to know about their mom in heaven. Give examples of ways you might choose to tell small children about the place where their loved ones are waiting.

SUSPENSE

RIVETING INSPIRATIONAL ROMANCE

Watch for our new series of
edge-of-your-seat suspense novels.
These contemporary tales
of intrigue and romance
feature Christian characters
facing challenges to their faith...
and their lives!

Steeple
Hill®

Visit:
www.SteepleHill.com

LISUSDIR07R

INSPIRATIONAL HISTORICAL ROMANCE

Engaging stories of romance,
adventure and faith,
these novels are set in
various historical periods
from biblical times
to World War II.

NOW AVAILABLE!

**Steeple
Hill®**

For exciting stories that reflect traditional values,
visit:
www.SteepleHill.com